I0743224

Love Forever on the Frontier

Based on the Life of William Bixby and His Family

CYNTHIA M. B. DRAYER

ISBN: 978-1-962363-01-3 (sc)
ISBN: 978-1-962363-02-0 (e)

Rev. date: 09/11/2023

Preface

This book has been a seventeen-year-long journey that began when I first heard of the story of Humpback Woman, a member of the Northern Cheyenne Tribe. Humpback Woman's story is one of heartache and of joy, ranging from her freedom on the open plains to her life in the Southern Cheyenne Tribe, her survival of the Sand Creek Massacre, her life interacting with the forts of Wyoming, and her confinement on the Tongue River Reservation (now called the Northern Cheyenne Reservation) in Montana. Her two youngest grandchildren, Sally and Jessie, and her great-grandchild Lucy all married White men who were close friends. These men were William Bixby, George Harris, and Albert Spang. William's parents were pioneers of Indiana and Iowa, and his brother-in-law was also a pioneer in Iowa. The story of his family parallels that of Humpback Woman throughout the book, until the marriages happen and the families start to live together.

William's sister, Mary Adeline Bixby, married Oliver Hazzard Perry Reed, whose parents were members of Jesus Christ of Latter-Day Saints (a.k.a. Mormons). Their love for each other shows the joys and hardships they experienced during the Civil War. Other members of William's family also go into the Civil War, but only one comes back home. As William matures, he joins the Army and is sent by train to build a new fort, Fort Fetterman, on the Platte River. It is here that William meets his best friend, George Harris, who has traveled from England. Together they have experiences at another fort built at the same time, Fort D.A. Russell, and interact with Fort Laramie. It is here that George meets and falls in love with the Indian Sally. William meets her sister Jessie, and eventually, they both marry and live on Crazy Creek River in Wyoming. They build a stagecoach stop with an inn so they can feed the hungry passengers. Eventually, they needed help and hired Albert Spang. When he meets Sally's daughter, Lucy, it was love at first sight. They all lived together at the inn and started to raise their many children. Always looking for ways to earn money for their family, the three friends went into cattle ranching. In the late 1880s, large cattle ranchers began a war against small cattle ranchers, which included William, George, and Albert. Tensions began to rise as hired guns were brought in. It was during this time that head members of the Northern Cheyenne Tribe came to the three Indian wives and asked them to move to the new Tongue River Reservation in Wyoming. All three families left Wyoming for the perilous trip to Lame Deer, Montana. Each of the White men were adopted into the tribe, along with all their children, thus becoming "White Indians." They were given lands for ranching, and they settled their families on the reservation.

The book starts with William Bixby's children trying to get him to a hospital. He has come down with a terrible affliction, and they are rushing him to a hospital in Sheridan, Wyoming, many miles from their ranch in Montana. It is October of 1918, and many people have come down with this mysterious illness. Many people are dying. I finished writing this book about five years ago. At that time, the Spanish Flu was one of the worst pandemics to hit the world. But as 2020 came about, the COVID-19 virus hit the world. As I look back at William's struggle to stay alive, I can imagine how hard it was to survive the Spanish Flu, as there were limited resources, little medicine, and no ventilators to help patients in 1918.

As I researched the descendants of these three families, it became apparent that almost all the current living members of the Northern Cheyenne Tribe are related to them. This includes my grandchildren. They can be proud of their ancestors. A few years after I was told the story of Humpback Woman, the United States government acknowledged that the Sand Creek Massacre should never have happened. Monetary compensation was given to all descendants of Humpback Woman and to the descendants of other survivors of this terrible crime. I dedicate this book to the descendants of Humpback Woman.

Much of the information in this book is historical in nature, but as with any puzzle, some pieces were missing. It was then that I used fiction to fill in the gaps. I hope the readers will enjoy this book as much as I have enjoyed writing it.

Chapter 1

*Road from Kirby, Montana, to Sheridan,
Wyoming, October 17, 1918*

It is a cold day in Montana. Snow has fallen, but it is starting to melt. The sky is cloudy and gray. There is a wagon drawn by four horses. The driver, Edward Bixby, is a young man with a felt hat on, red plaid bandanna around his neck, boots, Levi's pants, and a thick pea green wool coat. He has a mix of both White and Indian features: short-cropped black hair and dark-brown eyes. He seems desperate to keep the horses running, onward and onward. From the looks of him, there is a sense of fear in his eyes, a feeling he is not used to. He speaks to the horses in a harsh tone, as if they understand, lashing them with the reins and whipping them. Next to Ed is his older brother, Benjamin. Although Ben is older, you can sense that if he were a little bit more experienced in driving the horses, he would be the one making them go faster. In the wagon, lying down is a White man, about seventy-four years old, tall and slim, with bright blue eyes and hints of the reddish-brown hair he used to have among the white, a bushy mustache, bushy eyebrows, his facial skin dried out and wrinkled by the harsh weather he has been forced to work in. On his head there is a black felt hat with a wide hatband made of leather with some Indian silver decorations. He is very ill, sweating and coughing. Blankets surround him, but it does not seem to give him comfort. His large farmer hands are being held by an older Indian woman to his right (his wife, Jessie), and a young Indian woman on his left (one of his daughters, Anna). Although his wife has a blanket over her head, he can still see her long black hair with hints of gray—the hair that he still cherishes. Her hands are older than her age, full of arthritis from hard work in the home. Sitting next to her is a young Indian woman (another daughter, Mary). On the other side of her are two more young Indian women (her other daughters, twins Hattie and Louise). Some are weeping, all with blankets wrapped around their bodies to try to keep the cold breeze off. When they talk, there is a cold mist that comes out, which lingers outside of their lips.

The young man at the reins of the horses is impatient; he wants them to go faster and faster, but this is an unimproved road with chuckholes. The wheels hit hard into them, and each time there is a moan from the man in the back. On the curves, along with the mud and slush from the snow, the wagon slightly banks and slides. The horses are wearing out. Their breath is also misting in the air, and white lather is forming under their harness. This is a run for the life of the man in the back of the wagon, and time is running out.

> JESSIE BIXBY. Oh, Bill, hold on. I don't think I
> can take care of everything without you. Ed's
> driving as fast as he can. Albert said it would
> only take about two hours to get from Kirby,
> Montana, to Sheridan, Wyoming. Once we
> get there, the doctor will take care of you and
> everything will be all right.

She takes a cloth from a small basin, wrings it out, and rubs Bill's sweating forehead. She looks scared but is trying not to cry or to scare her children. Life has always been hard, but now it is going to get harder. Anna, her daughter, looks up from her father to her mother.

> ANNA. Dad should never have come to our house
> the other day. I know he wanted to help. My
> baby, Frank, was so sick. I didn't know what to
> do! Dad just doted over him. He tried to keep

him cool when he was so hot and tried to give him honey when he coughed. You could see the look in his face, the deep sadness he had when the little one died. It all happened so quickly. And now Dad has the same thing. We just got done with my boy's funeral, and I could see that Dad was not feeling well. And then he collapsed right there by the grave site. I feel so bad. I just can't take it anymore!

She sobs uncontrollably.

> JESSIE. Quiet down! It was no one's fault. He just couldn't stand by and let your little one go without trying to help. You know that. He loves all his grandchildren. And besides, if it is anyone's fault, it's mine, because I insisted that he go see you.

> BEN BIXBY, *to his mother, Jessie.* Ma, we should be there in a few minutes. I think we crossed the border from Montana into Wyoming, and Sheridan should be up ahead real soon.

But Jessie could not hear this as there is too much noise coming from the wheels, the horses, and her children. There are some promising signs that they are close. As they start traveling on paved roads instead of mud, homes start coming into view. Then there are more homes, and finally the town can be seen in the distance. They are almost there. A look of hope and determination comes back into Jessie's eyes. The sky is starting to separate, and the sun is starting to come out. Icicles that were hanging on the roof edges are now dripping, and some snow is falling off tree branches. As they get into the main part of town, already the road is thick with muddy tracks of other wagons that have been there before. They cross over cable car tracks. It is then that they see the chaos in front of the Sheridan Hospital. There is a line of people, almost a mob, pleading with the doctor out front to look at their loved ones. The doctor is forty years old, of medium height, with strong arms and big hands. He has a full beard with mustache, and thin metal-framed glasses. He could have been a farmer, but he was given the opportunity to be a doctor instead. He has a beige outfit on, with a beige felt hat, pants, and vest. His tie is black, and his shirt is white. Outside, in wagons, on litters, in carriages, and in automobiles are very ill people, all with the same symptoms as William. Some are children, some are adults, and some are older family members. Some are obviously rich, while many are farmers and miners. As they get closer, they can hear the doctor talking.

> DOCTOR. We have to take everyone to a building
> that has been donated by Attorney Lonabaugh.
> We will be setting it up with thirty-three
> emergency beds. The hospital is full. We don't
> have enough room.

A man in blue jean coveralls approaches through the crowd. People part for him so he can get through, eyes looking at what is in his arms.

> SAM, *with child in his arms.* My God, Doctor, what
> is happening? Why are all these people here?

He looks down at his limp son in his arms. Fear and grief are in his eyes.

> SAM. Please help my son. He's all I have, after
> Margaret died last year…

His voice gets tight, and he looks up at the doctor with tears.

> DOCTOR. I know, Sam. I'll do everything I can.
> You know that.

As he looks down into the boy's sweating and moaning face, he pushes his glasses a little bit farther up his long nose, trying to figure out what this small child has, what they all have. He then swings his arm over to the southeast and points to a hillside near Grinnell Street.

> DOCTOR, *in a loud voice.* We need to head up
> there. Be careful. Form a line and don't rush.

With his doctor's bag, his four assistants, and a wagonful of supplies, he starts the trek up the road on the hillside to the location where the lawyer's building stands. The litters and the carriages and the wagons and the cars follow, forming a long line.

> DOCTOR, *to one of his assistants as they are walking*
> *up the hill.* There are already twenty patients,
> and I am afraid that we are going to have chaos
> and riots. What is happening? No one has ever
> seen this before. One minute their loved one is
> eating breakfast, and by evening they are at my
> doorstep. Yesterday, Benjamin Dotta, a worker
> from the mines, died. He was forty-five years
> old, for gosh sakes, and in good health to boot!
> The patients that are already in the hospital are
> not doing well. I'm afraid that most of them
> won't make it. Already rumors have started that
> anyone who catches this disease will die and that
> anyone helping them will die too. We better
> figure out what this is fast!

> ONE OF THE ASSISTANTS. Per your order, the
> mayor has closed all the schools, theaters, and
> public gatherings, so maybe that will stop this
> from spreading. Some feel that a really good rain
> or big storm will pull down whatever is in the air
> and people will stop getting sick. We just don't
> have anything at our disposal to help people from

catching this killer, and we don't seem to have any
control over who recovers and who dies.

> DOCTOR, *to assistants*. The only thing we have
> at our disposal that might help is the new
> medication aspirin. But we don't know what
> dosage to give that will truly help our patients.
> We may do more harm than good if we overdose
> our patients. Be sure to wear your masks and
> gloves at all times. If we get sick, then there will
> be no one to take care of these patients, and
> more will certainly die.

As the people arrive at the building, the double doors are opened
wide and the hospital equipment is quickly brought in.

> DOCTOR, to men in crowd. Please, every able-
> bodied man, please come help to set up the cots
> and medical equipment. The faster we can do
> this, the better for your loved ones. Ed and Ben
> are there, helping to set up the equipment and
> placing patients on the cots.

Ed could not help but notice the glares directed their way. It was this
way all his life, the looks, even from his own tribal members. Because
he is a "half-breed," he does not seem to belong anywhere. He could
sense that some would not even let him touch their loved ones even
though they need his help to lift them up. A well-dressed man is lifting
his father out of a car. Ed runs up to help, as he can tell the man is very
heavy. But he is repulsed.

> MAN, *to Ed*. No, thank you! Get away, young man!
> I can do this myself!

His eyes and actions show his disgust that Ed would even think of touching him or his father. Some don't say anything; they just shove his arms and hands away. Or there is a simple, rough push by a stranger while they are walking past each other down the hall, with a glare of hatred as they turn their head to stare. They want to see his reaction, to see if he would fight them. But he knows to ignore such things. There is no way he could win in this environment. He would only end up in jail. His mom and sisters now sit near his father's cot. Reservation blankets are still around their heads and body due to the cold. It would take a while to warm up the old building.

When most of the commotion is over, he walks out for a breath of fresh, cold air. His brother is nearby, walking on the lawn, leaving footprints in what little snow is left. He yells out his brother's name.

ED BIXBY. Hey, Ben!

He jumps over the porch railing and hits the ground. As he approaches, he notices his brother has a look of despair, with tears in his eyes. Seeing his brother coming, Ben turns his head and wipes the tears away with his sleeve as quickly as he can.

> BEN BIXBY, *to Ed*. I can't believe this is happening.
> Look at all these people! Are we all going to
> catch this…*and die?*

> ED, *to Ben*. Remember the story that Dad told us
> about his mom and dad?

> BEN, *to Ed*. Yeah, he certainly had it hard after that
> winter of 1859.

Chapter 2

Indiana, 1841

The forests are full of beautiful fall colors, and a horseman is riding up to a small wooden cabin. The horse is black, with a white marking down the middle of his forehead. He dismounts his horse, ties it up to a post, and walks up the steps, across a small porch, and unlatches a door. The young man rushes up to a young woman with three children playing around her.

> PERRY BIXBY, *William's father*. I got the land
> grant, Nancy! We can finally move from here to
> our new home. I've heard that Iowa is a fertile
> place, and there is a grand river for transporting
> our goods. It will be a whole new life for us and
> our kids.

He has a grin on his face, takes his hat off, throws it on the bed, and grabs his wife's face, kissing her tenderly. Then he grabs her around the waist and twirls her around. They both laugh.

> PERRY. Our property is in Lee County, Iowa, on
> land that used to be set aside for the Sac and
> Fox Indian Nation. I can't believe that the
> government had a treaty so that the half breeds
> from the heathens and British soldiers could live
> on this land. They told them to go to a different
> place to live, so most of them have left the

area and it should be safe enough for us. What
would they do with such fertile, productive, and
rich land? It would have been such a waste. It is
so beautiful, and there is already a cabin on it. I
can make it bigger for our family as it grows.

He gives his wife a sly grin. Nancy Johnston Bixby, William's mother,
is excited.

> NANCY. When can we leave, Perry? Can it be
> before winter sets in, or do we have to wait until
> spring?

> PERRY. We can leave right away! I'll start getting
> the wagon ready. We'll put in all our items that
> we can fit into it. The donkeys can pull the
> wagon with me and the kids. Blaze can carry
> you. I don't want you walking with that baby in
> your belly.

He places his hand on her extended belly and pulls his hand back
when he feels a kick.

> PERRY. My, but he's a big kicker.

> NANCY. Now, Perry, you know it could just as
> easily be a girl. Why, look at Mary. She was so
> active you thought for sure she was a boy!

He looks down at the three children playing. Mary is grabbing a toy
from her older brother. In protest, Mary pushes the older boy, James.

> MARY. My toy. Give it to me.

> JAMES. Man, you are such a tomboy! You should
> act like a girl, not like a boy.

In disgust, he walks to the other side of his parents. Mary shows pride in her ability to boss her older brother.

> PERRY. She's a strong one, that's for sure. Moving makes me think of Ohio, where we got married. It's hard to believe we have been on these eighty acres for three years. Seems just like yesterday, James was just a baby. Well, I better get things going. We should be able to leave in two days.

> NANCY. We'll be ready, won't we, kids?

She looks down at their smiling faces.

Mississippi River, Two Months Later, 1841

Their trek will take two months and will cover over four hundred miles. Rough roads, rain, and colder weather make for a difficult ride. They cross the Mississippi River in a ferry from Illinois and are enjoying the scenery of their new homeland, the state of Iowa. It is the largest river they have ever seen.

> PERRY. Look, kids, there is the Mississippi River. Isn't it grand? You'll never see another river so wide you can see all the barges carrying goods to market!

Mary and Aaron get too close to the underside of the railing and have to be pulled back by Perry.

> NANCY. Not too close to the railing, kids. You don't want to end up in the river. Is our land nearby the river, Perry?

> PERRY. Yep, we are very close to the river, but not too close. We won't have to worry about the

annual flooding, but we can go fishing every
day if we want to. And we are close enough to
Montrose so we can get supplies when we need
them.

After they get to shore, they start the wagon again until the sun starts
to set. The children are restless when they camp for yet another day.

MARY, *to Nancy*. I want to be there now, Mommy.
It's too cold and wet. I don't like this. When are
we going to be there? I *hate* camping!

Mary whimpers and pulls on her mother's dress, with a pouting look
on her face, her feet stomping. The youngest baby, Aaron, is on Nancy's
hip, crying for another feeding (again), which she can't provide yet. Her
belly is protruding, and her other hand is holding her back, which aches.

NANCY, *to Mary*. Mary Adaline Bixby, will you
stop complaining?

MARY. When I get older, I'm going to be called
Adaline. Mary is such a common name.

Nancy looks around with a worried look.

NANCY. Where did James go? That little rascal is
always exploring around. He is going to be in
big trouble when he gets back! I told him not to
leave the camp.

She walks over to Perry while he is feeding the animals.

NANCY, *to Perry*. Perry, have you seen James? I'm
worried. He's walked off again. Do you know
how much longer it will be? I'm soaking wet.

Some of the food got wet, and I don't think we
will be able to use it. What are we going to do?

The look on her face is one of worry, for the kids, for herself, for
Perry, and for her unborn baby. She wipes sweat off her brow. She knows
that life on the frontier is full of promise, but it is also full of worry,
hardships, hard work, and sometimes pain. They have not had a chance
to wash or bathe in days, and their faces and hands show that the days
have been full of mud.

> PERRY, *to Nancy*. Now, Nancy, don't get so upset. I
> saw James. He's just near that berry patch a few
> yards down the way. I think he is trying to get
> us some berries. That would be a nice treat. I'm
> pretty sure I can fish for some food if we travel
> along the river. Your brother Jesse is not far from
> here, and we can probably stop there to refresh
> ourselves before we head to our new home.
> Besides, it's all his fault that we are here. His
> story about this land is what got me so excited
> about coming here. The least he can do is to
> welcome us for a day or two.

> NANCY, *to Perry*. I'm so glad I'm your wife! You
> always take a problem and figure out a solution.
> And you are such a great father. How did I get
> so lucky? I love you!

Nancy starts to tickle her little boy, Aaron.

> NANCY, *to Aaron*. Isn't your daddy the best?

The baby laughs out loud and wiggles around in delight. Perry
gives Nancy a tender kiss on the cheek and returns to his duties with
the animals.

NANCY, *to Perry*. I'm going to walk down to the
berry patch and help James pick some berries.

James sees his mother approaching and expects a scolding. He hides the fact that there are berries loaded into his white shirt, which now has stained the color of the berries, dark red.

JAMES. Hey, Mom, now, don't get mad. I just
wanted to get us some food for dinner.

NANCY. I know, sweetie. You have a natural knack
for living in the frontier, unlike your sister. You
always make the best of a situation. You are
going to grow up into a fine young man, able
to take care of his family, just like your dad.
However…

She looks at her son with a disapproving look as she pulls Aaron higher on her hip.

NANCY. You need to stay nearby, where we can see
you. It hasn't been very long since the savages
were living here. There still might be some
nearby. I don't want anything to happen to you.
And next time, would you take a bucket so your
clothes don't get so stained. You know we don't
have many cloths to change into.

JAMES. Sorry, Mom.

He looks sheepish and knows that he's broken a rule.

JAMES. Why are we moving, Mom? I liked our
home. Why did we leave it? I'd like to go back.

NANCY. Your father got a land grant in Iowa, and
　　　it is a big opportunity for us to start a farm on
　　　fertile land. The farm we had was rocky, hard
　　　to weed, there was not enough water, and there
　　　wasn't an easy way for us to sell our produce.
　　　Our home was too small for the five of us. So
　　　now we will have a better life. Why, going West
　　　is the American dream!

She grins and places her arm around him.

NANCY. It's time to go back up toward the wagon.
　　　I have to make dinner, and I want you nearby.
　　　I think you have enough berries. I'll put them
　　　on the biscuits special so we can all have some.
　　　Come on, let's go.

They both head back. Mary is talking to herself about the hardships
and is glad to see her mother arrive with James. She runs up and starts
a torrent of complaints, and Nancy rolls her eyes. Later, after Nancy
prepares the meal, she is serving the biscuits for her family.

NANCY. Well, as you can see, we have a special
　　　treat tonight. James was able to pick these
　　　berries to brighten up our meal. Thank you,
　　　son. You did good.

She grins as only a mother can grin to her son when she is so proud
of him.

PERRY. These berries are so sweet!

JAMES. Glad I could help.

He is beaming with a big smile. Mary is eating the sweet berries
quickly.

MARY. I think I see a bug on this berry. Uhhhg!
Wait, it's half a bug…what happened to the
other half?

She looks up with her face questioning what she is seeing, looking for an answer among her family members. They all look over at Mary with the same thought: she has eaten half of the bug. They burst out in laughter.

Jesse Johnston's Farm, Two Days Later

Two days after entering Iowa, the family finally sees the home of Nancy's brother, Jesse. As they approach, chickens begin to scatter. There is a corral with two horses, and another pen with pigs. A medium-size dog has started to bark. Jesse is doing well. Jesse's wife, Maria, runs out. She has recognized the people riding in.

MARIA JOHNSTON. Oh my gosh, I can't believe
it is you! Jesse will be so excited when he sees
you! He's out in the fields right now, getting
ready for a harvest.

As she wipes her hands off with her apron, she runs up and helps Nancy off the horse. As they walk to the porch, she starts a conversation.

MARIA, *to Nancy*. I see you are getting ready for
another baby. Congratulations! You must be
tired, and it looks like you have been introduced
to the famous Iowa mud!

She grins and makes a slight laugh as she places her arm under Nancy's arm in friendship.

> NANCY, *to Maria.* You look great, Maria, just like you did when I saw you on your wedding day to my brother.

> MARIA. Hush now, you are telling lies. We have three babies now, just like you and Perry. Come on in. Be careful of that last step. It needs some repairing.

Perry and the children have gotten off the wagon and have followed Maria and Nancy into the house. It is comfortable enough, with a stove for cooking, along with a fireplace, and two bedrooms. There is furniture to sit on, a nice table with chairs to eat at. Three young children run out to meet their cousins. Soon all the family is clean and dressed in dry clothing.

> MARIA. As you can see, the weather down in southern Iowa is pretty wet. And the mud sticks to you like paint. You are staying for dinner and overnight. I won't think of anything else.

> NANCY, *to Maria.* Well, we could use a little break from camping on the ground. Thank you so much.

Just then, a big stomping can be heard on the porch, the door latch is opened, and in comes a burly man. Although he has tried to stomp out mud from his boots, they are still muddy, up through the cuffs of his coveralls. When he sees Perry and Nancy, he runs up to Nancy and gives her a big hug while twirling her around.

> JESSE, to Nancy. Sis, it is so great to see you! I heard that Perry had decided to take my advice and move out here. It is the best land, and the new settlers here are real friendly. Why, you only

see a few Indians around, usually in the town of
Montrose. They're usually drunk in the streets,
or in jail. No threat to us at all. You and Perry
are going to find this a great place to live.

Jesse looks at his wife, Maria, and talks to her in a scolding manner,
with a finger pointing to her.

JESSE, *to Maria.* Why didn't you come to get me
when they arrived?

MARIA. Oh, now, Jesse, you needed to get the
harvest in, and they're going to stay at least
overnight. You'll have plenty of time to visit.

There is a hearty meal of freshly hunted deer and biscuits, and even
some vegetables and fruits from their garden. It is the best meal they
have had since leaving Indiana two months ago.

JESSE, *to Perry.* I want you to know that I shot that
deer myself not more than one hundred yards
from the front door. Why, there is enough wild
food out here to last a lifetime! And you can see
that we can have a garden with fresh fruits and
vegetables. The extra we can sell, or they can be
canned for the wintertime by Maria. She is a
wonderful woman, that Maria of mine.

He sends a sly look to his wife, who is obviously proud that her
husband thinks so highly of her talents in the household. At the end of
the meal, Maria and Nancy pick up all the dishes and food from the
table while Jesse gets out a fiddle.

JESSE. Hey, folks, let's have a little hoedown.

He starts to play some quickstep dancing tunes. The whole group starts clapping their hands and slapping their knees. The fireplace gives a background of flickering light. Some of the young kids even begin to dance, sometimes stomping their feet in rhythm with the music, giving out shouts of glee and laughter. Then after all the excitement, the children are all put to sleep.

> NANCY, *to Maria and Jesse.* Thank you so much for
> the great hospitality, meal, and fun. Perry and I
> haven't been able to really relax this whole trip.

> MARIA. I remember when Jesse and I came out
> from Ohio. It was a long, hard trip. But you will
> see that it was worth all the worry.

That night, while Nancy and Perry are rested and ready for bed, they have a small conversation.

> PERRY. Hard to believe we are almost there. It has
> been quite a trip! You and the kids have put
> up with a lot. I'm proud of the way you have
> handled all the hardship along the way.

> NANCY. I would follow you anywhere, Perry. You
> are my life, my love, and I can't think of being
> without you. This will be the beginning of a
> whole new life for us.

Cabin, Lee County, Iowa, Two Days Later

Finally, the wagon is arriving at their new home in Lee County, Iowa. A cabin stands to the right as the wagon turns to get in front of the porch. Nancy looks ill. After all, it has been a hard trip from Indiana to Iowa. The sun has been out but is now starting to set, and a lot of leaves have fallen from the trees onto the ground. Birds are singing in the meadow nearby. The kids are all excited and, once out of the wagon, begin to shout and run around, looking at the trees and the house. The leaves make crushing noises under their feet. They pick some up and throw them at one another. Shouts of protest can be heard between the laughter when leaves hit their faces. The youngest, Aaron, has just learned to walk and falls often. Although he has learned how to get back up on his own, it is Mary who turns around to help him get back up. She is his protector.

> MARY, *with her stern finger*. Cyrus Aaron Bixby,
>   you need to be more careful. Now, don't fall
>   again. Let me help you up.

She reaches down as Aaron reaches up to her, a grin on his face, and they run off toward James.

Perry helps Nancy down from the horse and helps her into the cabin. Other than a few leaves, dirt, and dust, there is nothing in the cabin. It is totally empty and dark. Some windowpanes are broken. There is no firewood for the fireplace, and there is a chill in the air, with a brisk wind filtering through the cracks between the boards.

An occasional knothole lets some light in along with another blast of cold air.

> NANCY. Perry, something isn't right. I'm not
>   feeling well. I think you need to get a doctor.
>   Maybe the neighbor down the road, the one we
>   just passed, maybe they can help you find where
>   the doctor is…

Her voice trails off as a wave of pain comes over her and she grabs her belly. Her stance sways a little. Grabbing her, he pulls her over to the wall to steady her.

> PERRY. Stand here, I'll get the mattress so you can
>   lie down.

He leaves the cabin, and you can hear noises as he lifts several items out of the wagon until he can get to the mattress and a blanket. Then he has to lift it out and carry it into the cabin. With much effort he lays it down in a corner along a wall and starts to help Nancy down so she can lie down. She cringes with pain and discomfort but calms a little once she gets totally down. He lays the blanket over her.

> PERRY. I'll get some firewood and start a fire. Then
> I'll get the kids in, and they will need to stay
> inside until I get back. I'll go get the doctor.

You can tell he has great anxiety for his wife. He rushes out of the cabin, grabs the ax that he has already taken out of the wagon, and begins to locate dry wood that he could use for the fire. Taking it in as quickly as he could, he places a few small pieces of wood at the bottom, lays most of the larger wood in the fireplace, and strikes a match that he has taken from his pocket. The fire starts slowly and then picks up to provide warmth and light. Perry looks over at Nancy and then sees that all three children have come in from outside and are looking at her. He instructs the children.

> PERRY. Now you need to stay in the house. Your
> mommy will be here, but I have to leave and
> should be back soon. Stay away from the fire. I
> don't want any of you to get hurt. Don't open
> the door until I get back. Is that understood?

Mary wags her head in a nod. Perry grabs the kids and hugs them, and then he bends down to Nancy and gives her a kiss on the cheek.

> PERRY, *to Nancy.* Be back as soon as I can. Don't
> worry, you're probably just tired from all the
> riding and camping we had to do to get here.
> Love you!

He gets back up and runs out the door. You can hear the wagon leaving, with noises from the donkeys and wheels running over the dirt. Two hours later, Perry is back; you can hear the donkeys bray and the wagon wheels and chains knock against the backboard.

> PERRY. Here it is, Doc. We just got here today,
> and Nancy is feeling real bad. We need to hurry
> inside.

You can hear the creaking of the wagon as they both jump down. The doctor and Perry rush inside the door. The three children are huddled over by what is left of the fire, holding one another and watching their mother. Nancy is moaning in pain. Perry runs over to the fireplace and throws in more wood, which adds much-needed warmth and some light. Quickly Perry introduces the doctor.

> PERRY, *to Nancy*. Here's the doctor, Nancy. His
> name is Hiram Jones.

The doctor can see that Nancy is unable to shake his hand and gets down to business.

> DR. JONES, *to Nancy*. Nice to meet you, Mrs.
> Bixby. Let's see what is going on here.

The doctor gets on his knees and lifts the blanket and Nancy's skirt. He is upset.

> DR. JONES. You need to push right now. The baby
> is already coming!

But she is so exhausted there is no strength left. Perry gets on his knees by her side and lifts her head and her back up.

> PERRY. Push, Nancy. The doctor needs you to
> push. The baby is almost here! You need to help

him. Come on, honey, you can do this. I'm here
now to help.

Nancy screams in agony as she tries to push. Again and again and again she pushes, then finally, the baby is here. But there is no crying, no movement from the baby. It is too early. The baby is dead.

DOCTOR. I'm sorry, the baby is not breathing. It
was a boy.

Perry buries his head against Nancy's and they cry together. Perry was right; it had been a boy. This is not the first baby they have lost, but they are just as heartbroken as they were with the first. Their happy move into Iowa has started with disaster for the family. It is a bad omen.

Chapter 3

Iowa, 1846

As time passes, the house is improved and the family grows. There are James, Mary, and Aaron, as well as Benjamin and William. The view from their farm faces the Mississippi River, and they could see the developing town of Nauvoo, Illinois, which is being settled by the new religious group the Church of Jesus Christ of Latter-Day Saints. Everyone calls them Mormons. By 1844, there are fifteen thousand people living in Nauvoo, and it becomes the biggest city in Illinois. But a controversy begins and violence against the Mormons spreads throughout Illinois. The Mayor and religious leader Joseph Smith and his brother Hyrum are murdered by a mob while being held in a jail in Carthage, Illinois. Many inhabitants of Nauvoo begin fleeing to a new homeland in Utah, which is part of Mexico. But some of the followers of Joseph Smith's son, Joseph Smith III, settle into southern Iowa.

For many months now, the Mormons have been crossing the Mississippi from Illinois into Iowa on their trek to Utah. Many of them are ill prepared for the journey and need help from people they meet along the way. One day, a woman with a Mormon hand cart and two children cross Perry's property.

> PERRY. Here, let me help you. That journey across
> the great river must have been exhausting. Let
> me get you some water, and some food.

WOMAN, *with a hand cart and two small children.*
It's a terrible day, but the future will be much
brighter. We are going to settle in Utah, so we
will be safe. We can't believe that our leader
and mayor, Joseph Smith, was murdered by
that mob! And his brother, Hyrum, also. They
were so close, those two brothers. They are true
martyrs. It is kind of you to give us so much
help when so many on the other side of the river
have given us such hardship.

Nancy has come out of the home, with some of her children following
her, wiping her hands on her apron as she approaches with a dish of
food and a glass of water. The woman eats some of the food quickly
and then shares some with her children. She drinks the water as if she
has not had some for quite some time, then gives some to her children.

NANCY. I hear that some of you will be staying in
Iowa.

WOMAN. Yes. Joseph's son, Joseph Smith III, has
decided to stay with some of the other followers
and they are going to settle in Iowa. I wish them
well, but I believe that Bingham Young is the
true leader of our group, so I am following him
to Utah. Come on, kids, we have a long, long
way to walk. We are going to join a whole group
of our followers, and then we are going to walk
the wilderness together. It should be quite an
adventure!

She brushes the food off her mouth with the back of her hand and
starts to pull the cart, with her children walking behind.
Nancy places her arm around Perry.

NANCY. I remember what it was like to look
forward to a new place and a new future with
hope that it would be better. Well, I better get
back into the house to make dinner. Come on,
kids, let's go back into the house.

She walks slowly from Perry into their home.

Montrose, Iowa, 1858

Several years have passed and Mary is talking to Oliver Hazzard Perry
Reed, her fiancé. Oliver's parents came from New York and were followers
of the Mormon faith. He faces discrimination from his neighbors. He
is slender, with a brown coat, a light-brown vest and pants, and black
shoes. A gold fob holds a gold watch. He has a small mustache and bushy
eyebrows. He is a little older than Mary and has been in business for
several years. He is doing well and is quite wealthy. Mary has matured
into a beautiful young woman, red hair curled down her shoulders,
and blue eyes, in a tight, corseted dress with hoops underneath. She is
now called Adaline instead of Mary, which is the name that both Mary
and Oliver prefer. They are standing together in a gazebo at a park in
Montrose, Iowa. It is a sunny afternoon, and the birds are singing.

ADALINE. Oliver, I don't care that your family
is Mormon. I've seen how some of the
townspeople treat you with distaste, especially
when they found out about the Mormons in
Utah having multiple wives. But the followers
of Joseph Smith's son are different. They believe
that you marry one person for life. I can handle
this. Together we will make a difference. We will
show this town together what type of person
you are, what type of couple we can be. We love
each other, and I do not want any other man.
I'm stronger than you think.

She looks adoringly at Oliver, expressing her commitment and desire for him. She places her two hands on his shoulders, and he places his hands on her cheeks. He kisses her with relief, knowing that she will marry him.

> OLIVER. I don't know how I ever found you,
> Adaline. You are so wonderful. Most of my life
> I have been struggling to express my faith in a
> community that can't seem to accept it. For a
> country that was founded on religious freedom,
> in America I find that there is only freedom
> if you believe as they do. If you believe any
> differently, you are excluded from society. You
> are an outcast.

Oliver calms down and looks down at Adaline.

> OLIVER. When I look into your eyes and feel
> your touch, I know we will be able to survive
> anything that comes our way. Let's get married
> right away. I don't want to spend another day
> apart from you!

He smiles and grabs her tightly as she closes her eyes and embraces him. After a few seconds, she pulls away with a worried look on her face.

> ADALINE. You know, Oliver, we can't get married
> right away unless you ask for my hand in
> marriage from my father. It is important and
> shows respect.

> OLIVER. I'll do it right away. Tomorrow is Sunday
> and he will be out of the fields. I will come over
> then.

> ADALINE. Okay, I'll see you then.

Perry's Home

Perry's home is much improved since they first moved in. There is a stove and a fireplace. There are four extra rooms and furniture for all the family members to eat a meal. In the back is a barn with animals and storage for hay. Now there are eight children, including Elizabeth, Lewis, and the toddler, Jackson. Nancy, as always, is preparing a meal for everyone. Adaline is nervous, knowing that Oliver will be there any minute to see her father. It is a big moment. She is not sure her father will accept Oliver, because of his faith.

Perry is sitting in a chair on the porch, whittling on a piece of wood. The sharp knife slices against the wood, forming long pieces that fall away onto the porch. As he is sitting there, Oliver arrives on his white stallion. Its hair is well groomed, its bridle shiny; the saddle is of the finest leather. Oliver gets off and wraps the reins around a post. He walks up to Perry.

> OLIVER. Hello, Mr. Bixby. May I pull up a chair
> and talk with you for a little?

Perry nods in agreement as he continues to whittle. Oliver drags a wooden chair from the other side of the porch up to where Perry is sitting. Adaline has heard the noise and is sneaking a peek out of the window, hoping that no one will see her. But Nancy sees her daughter's move to the window and figures out that something important is about to happen. She takes a big breath and holds the wooden mixing spoon close to her heart in anticipation.

> OLIVER. Mr. Bixby, you know that I have been
> seeing your daughter Adaline. We have grown
> very close these past few months. You also know
> that I have a small business in Montrose that
> is doing very well, and that I have a wonderful
> house. I could provide for her. I'm here, Mr.

Bixby, to ask for…both hands of Adaline. I
don't just want one. I want both of them.

Oliver has a smile on his face and is hoping that Perry will understand
the joke (both hands instead of one). Perry's face shows the reaction he
is looking for, a laugh in his voice and glee in his eyes. The whittling has
stopped, and Perry has gotten up, followed by Oliver, from his chair. As
Perry reaches for and grabs Oliver's hand, he is heard to say something.

PERRY. I would be happy to have you as my son
in-law. You have my permission to marry my
daughter. And please call me Perry. Mr. Bixby is
way too formal for family.

Adaline can't contain her happiness and gives out a squeal as she
realizes that she is going to be Mrs. Reed. She runs up to her mother
and gives her a hug, and Nancy responds by hugging her. Her little
baby is grown up and going to become a wife, and probably a mother.
It is something that every parent looks forward to. Happiness in their
children, with a firm future.

Adaline runs out of the front door, and Oliver turns and sees her.
He steps forward, and they have a long, loving kiss. The other kids in
the house say, "Get a room!" and give disgusting noises at having to see
their older sister kissing.

Marriage Ceremony, Montrose, Iowa, October 13, 1858

Because of Temple rules, only members of the faith can attend the
wedding inside. This meant that all of Adaline's family had to wait
outside. Oliver and Adaline are hand in hand, facing each other, as they
are sealed together forever.

OFFICATING APOSTLE. Do you, Mary Adaline
Bixby, take Oliver Hazzard Perry Reed as your
lawfully wedded husband, to have and to hold,
for all eternity?

ADALINE. Yes, I do.

OFFICIAL. Do you, Oliver Hazzard Perry Reed,
    take Mary Adaline Bixby as your lawfully
    wedded wife, to have and to hold, for all
    eternity?

OLIVER. Yes, I do.

OFFICIAL. I now pronounce you man and wife!
    You may kiss the bride!"

Oliver takes Adaline and tenderly kisses his wife. They run down the steps of the temple, happy, with their family throwing rice.

Montrose, Lee County, Iowa,
Nine Months Later, July 3, 1859

A happy event is occurring, as Adaline has conceived her first child and has begun her labor. The brothers and sister and her father are all downstairs. Her mother, Nancy, is upstairs with her. Oliver is walking the floors, listening to the noises from Adaline as she pushes their baby into the world. Oliver has a cigar in his mouth, nervously takes it out, and then puts it back in. Then there is the noise of a baby's cry. There is a rush to the bottom of the stairs as Dr. Smith comes out to give them the news.

DR. SMITH, *at top of stairs.* Well, Oliver, it's a
    healthy baby boy! And he has one of the loudest
    cries I have ever heard!

The news is met with resounding happiness among the family members present. Oliver starts handing out cigars that were hiding in the inside of his coat pocket. He hands them out haphazardly, even to those that are way too young to smoke. He looks up.

OLIVER. Can I see them now?

DOCTOR. Yes. Come up.

Oliver rushes up, two steps at a time, but as he makes the landing, the doctor pulls him over and whispers something in his ear.

> DOCTOR. Oliver, there was some complication
> during the delivery. The baby was in the wrong
> position. We had to do a procedure to help the
> baby come out, but Adaline is bleeding, and we
> are having a hard time stopping it. She is weak,
> so only stay a few minutes, and let her sleep.

Oliver opens the door slowly and enters. Adaline is in bed, with the baby beside her. Her mother, Nancy, is standing by to help with whatever is needed. He approaches Nancy and pulls her aside. He whispers to her, a worried look on his face.

> OLIVER. The doctor says it was a tough delivery.
> You think she'll be okay?

> NANCY. My babies usually came so easy. It was
> hard to see my daughter go through so much.
> But we are here to help her, so she should come
> out of this.

Oliver walks over to Adaline, his heart beating rapidly as he sees his son up close for the first time. Adaline looks so weak, but the baby is active, moving his arms and head.

> OLIVER, *to Adaline.* Hello, honey, how are you
> doing? Look at that little bundle of joy!

He reaches down to tickle the baby on the chin. He has dark blue eyes and brownish-red hair, just enough to cover some of his head.

OLIVER. I was told to only be here for a few
    minutes, to give you rest. Your mom will be
    here to help out if you need anything. I'm right
    downstairs with the whole family. They're all
    excited for us!

ADALINE, *to mom*. Oliver and I decided to name
    the baby Walter if it was a boy.

Oliver nods in agreement. She sighs and looks tired, unable to really
even hold her own newborn.

ADALINE, *to Oliver*. The whole family is
    downstairs? Go ahead and take him down so I
    can get a little rest.

Adaline turns her head away as Nancy takes the baby. She and Oliver
leave the bedroom. They walk down the stairs.

NANCY, *to Oliver*. I'm really worried. This is not
    like Adaline. She was so excited about this baby
    coming. She must be feeling really bad to turn
    him over to us.

As they hit the bottom of the stairs, the family members are all
over them.

OLIVER, *to family*. His name is Walter.

AARON, *to William*. Why, William, look, he has
    your hair color and eyes!

ELIZABETH, *to her father*. Wow, Dad, he has your
    ears and nose.

Perry places his arms around Nancy as he looks into the face of their first grandchild.

> PERRY, *to Nancy*. This is what it's all about,
> providing for your family so that they can, in
> turn, provide for theirs.

> PERRY, *to Oliver*. Congratulations, Oliver! You
> have a wonderful little guy.

> OLIVER. How does it feel like to be grandparents?

> PERRY AND NANCY, *together*. Wonderful!

Chapter 4

Perry's Cabin, Iowa, December 1859

It is only five months after Adaline's baby was born. There are two people, Perry and Nancy, in beds that are at forty-five-degree angles from each other. They are both sweating and coughing. Their eight children are three to twenty-three years old. The older children, James, Adaline, and Aaron, are trying to help with washbasins and washcloths to place them on their parents' foreheads. The younger children, Benjamin, William, Elizabeth, Lewis, and Jackson, are nearby, scared. Nancy is trying to talk with Perry.

> NANCY. Perry, you still there? You need to fight
> this thing. Can you hear me?

She reaches over to try to touch his hand as one of his arms is hanging outside of the bed limp and pale. He is too far away. Perry is starting to cough harder and wheezing. And then, it stops. He goes limp. His breath has stopped. His eyes are open but do not blink. James backs off in horror. Aaron looks up and drops the washcloth back into his mother's water basin. Adaline screams and holds her dad, burying her head into his chest.

> ADALINE. No, Daddy, don't go! Come back…

Sobs and tears combine with great pain in her breathing. She is heartbroken. The other children start to cry in agony and great sadness, and their mother hears their pain.

NANCY. My dear, sweet husband, I can't live
    without you…

Nancy goes into a coma-like state. She has given up the fight for life. Although the children continue their efforts to save their mother, she, too, comes to the end of life. As they stand by the bodies of their parents, Adaline pulls James and Aaron into a huddle. Although bewildered by their parents' sudden death, they need to act quickly for the family, to keep it together.

ADALINE, *to James and Aaron.* I'm not sure what
    we can do. James, you should stay on the farm
    and see if we can lease it out or sell it. Hiram
    and Lodenna Scranton have been here, asking
    about our farm, and they might buy it. We have
    to take care of the younger kids. Benjamin is
    seventeen, and William is fourteen. I think our
    uncle and aunt Jesse and Maria Johnston could
    put Benjamin to work on their farm. They
    would probably treat him like their son rather
    than a hired hand. For William, he could live
    with our neighbors Alonzo and Jennie Crandel.
    They have always liked William, and he has
    helped them on their farm before. Maybe they
    can take him in in exchange for room and
    board. He would be close enough to me. That
    just leaves the younger ones. I think Oliver and
    I can put up the younger children, Elizabeth,
    Lewis, and Jackson. Aaron, you may need to
    help me with the younger kids since I have

Walter to look out for. I'll need help from you two for some income. Are you in agreement?

JAMES. You bet, sis. We can help out. Don't you worry.

AARON. Same here.

ADALINE. Dad and Mom didn't talk much about their finances and debts, and I don't think they had a will. We are going to need help. This winter was so bad I think most of our animals are going to die. We just don't have enough feed for them due to the drought this summer. Everyone is in the same situation. We may have to sell the farm in order to pay off our debts. I hope we can hold off any other hardships.

JAMES. With all the primaries and the elections next year, I'm thinking that Abraham Lincoln will become President. My fear is that a war will start between us and our neighboring states if that happens.

ADALINE. We've got to keep our family together. It is what Mom and Dad would have wanted.

Tears come to Adaline's eyes, and she wipes them away. James and Aaron give her a hug and put their arms around her. Soon the smaller children are together with them, all crying. It is a moment that none of them will forget.

JAMES. We can do this together. We'll stay together.

Back to Sheridan, Wyoming, 1918

Ed and Ben are still talking outside in the melting snow. It is now afternoon, and the sun is high in the sky.

> ED, *to Ben.* I'm glad that our grandparents got to see their first grandchild before they died. I bet it meant a lot to them, just like it did to Mom and Dad when sister Mary gave birth to her first child.

> BEN, *to Ed.* Yeah, it certainly was a happy time. But from the stories that Dad told, there were more hardships ahead. Death was all around them…

Chapter 5

Montrose, Iowa, 1860

As promised, Adaline and her husband, Oliver, have taken in her brother Aaron and her younger brothers and sister. Her other brothers are out on surrounding farms.

The primaries and debates are in full swing for the election of the next President. The Southern states have threatened to succeed if Abraham Lincoln is elected. Slave states and non-slave states are already looking at what they will do and what men will fight for. Men graduating from West Point will also be choosing sides.

July of 1860 is a census year, and the agents go through Iowa. As predicted, there are Oliver Reed; his wife, Adaline; and their son, Walter. In his household are Adaline's siblings Aaron, Lewis, Elizabeth, and Jackson. William is with Alonzo Crandel's family next door. James is on the old farm with Hiram Scranton and his family. Benjamin is farther away with their uncle Jesse Johnston.

Oliver Reed's Home, Montrose, Iowa
Early Morning, October 12, 1860

In the early morning, there is a lot of activity before breakfast as Oliver is getting ready for work. Adaline is getting the children ready and then will be preparing breakfast for them all. Lewis and Elizabeth are getting ready for school. Jackson is just being himself, full of mischief.

ADALINE, *to Lewis and Elizabeth*. Hurry up, you
two. You are going to be late for school. Take a
sweater as the weather is looking a little colder
today. And this time, don't forget your slates and
lunch.

You can hear Elizabeth yelling from her bedroom.

ELIZABETH, *to Adaline*. I can't find my shoes!
Where are my brown shoes? I have to have them
or I will just die. I need my shoes to match my
brown skirt!

She leans down and looks under her bed. Adaline is in the baby's
room with Walter, changing his diaper. Lewis is in his room, one he
shares with his brother Jackson.

LEWIS, *calling out to Adaline*. Hey, sis, where is
the strap for my book and slate? I think I saw
Jackson playing with it.

ADALINE, *to Lewis*. Yeah, I saw it in the closet.

Jackson has toddled into the baby's room and is starting to play with
the talcum powder, getting it all over. Adaline grabs it away.

ADALINE, *to Jackson*. No, Jackson, not for you.
For baby.

Jackson reaches up for Adaline to pick him up, but she is not done
with Walter. Soon after Walter is done, she grabs him up, grabs Jackson,
and with one child on each hip, heads to the kitchen. Into high chairs
they go, and she starts breakfast. Jackson is protesting; he wants out of
the high chair, but Adaline has learned the hard way what can happen
when Jackson is roaming around on his own.

ADALINE, *to Jackson*. Stop protesting, Jack. You
know you have to be in the high chair.

JACKSON, *to Adaline*. Help me out! I want out!

Adaline raises his right hand and shows him a big scar.

ADALINE, *to Jackson*. No, baby gets hurt!

Adaline has always wanted to be a mom, but not to four little kids at
once. Breakfast is almost done. Now she needs to let the whole household
know.

ADALINE, *yelling*. Breakfast is almost done! Aaron,
can you put the plates and silverware on the
table?

AARON. Sure, Adaline.

She has Aaron place the plates, glasses, and utensils on the table,
and then kids start rushing into the kitchen to get seated. It is a large
rectangular oak table surrounded by oak chairs with high backs. Padding
is on each chair for comfort. There is a large pane of glass that looks out
into the backyard. They can see the green grass, the last of the flowers,
and the trees have just about finished dropping their colorful leaves.
Birds can be heard chirping through the crisp air and blue skies. They
are all seated at the table, except for Oliver. Oliver's empty chair is at
one end, and Adaline's is at the other. The two young boys are in high
chairs on each side of Adaline so she can help them eat. Oliver finally
comes down. You can hear his steps down the stairs. He walks through
the living room and into the kitchen. He bends over and gives Adaline
a kiss on her cheek, gives a kiss to his little boy, Walter, on the head,
and reaches over to give a pat on Jackson's head.

OLIVER. Good morning to you all. That's what
    I like to see, everyone happy and healthy and
    ready to start the day!

He sits at his chair and says a quick prayer of thanks for the food, then places a napkin on his lap. As he starts to dig in and pass food around, the others begin fighting for their share of the food. As they finish, Lewis and Elizabeth get up to grab their schoolbooks, slates, and lunches. Aaron gets up to escort them to school. You can hear scuffling on the floor in the front room and the front door opening.

KIDS, *to Adaline and Oliver.* Bye!

The door closes. By now, Jackson is pretty much uncontrollable.

JACKSON. Me, out! Help me…HELP ME…!

He squirms and bounces in an effort to get himself out. Adaline gives up and lets him out. He scurries out into the front room. She starts to collect the dishes, glasses, etc. and takes them to the kitchen sink. Oliver gets up with her and walks to the sink, carrying some of the leftover dishes. Adaline looks at Oliver in surprise.

ADALINE, *to Oliver.* Aren't you going to be late for
    work?

OLIVER. Well, I am the boss. I guess I can be late
    once in a while.

He laughs.

ADALINE. You've been so busy lately we haven't
    had much time to talk. You've taken on so much
    responsibility, both at work and here at home.
    I really appreciate you helping my brothers and
    sister.

She looks down in apprehension, then looks back up.

> ADALINE. Oliver, I'm pregnant again. I've had
> a hard time telling you. It's just all a little
> overwhelming…

Tears are starting to come to her eyes, and she is starting to shake. Oliver immediately grabs her in joy.

> OLIVER. Oh, Adeline, how wonderful! Don't
> worry, maybe if business does a little better, I
> can hire a maid to help you with Walter and the
> meals.

> ADALINE. Oh, Oliver, I was afraid you would be
> upset with another baby in the household! I'm
> so glad you are happy. Do you think we could
> get a maid? I sometimes think that if you work
> just one more minute, it is going to kill you.
> You're so exhausted when you come home.

Her eyes look up into his, and he hugs her and kisses her.

> OLIVER. You know, our second anniversary is
> tomorrow, and I want to do something really
> special. I want to meet you at the gazebo at the
> park. I'm going to have a special lunch for us at
> twelve noon to celebrate our special day. After
> all, it was there that you told me you would be
> my wife. It was the happiest day of my life!

Adeline presses her head against his chest.

> OLIVER. I was going to save this for tomorrow,
> but now that you have told me about the baby, I
> want to give it to you now.

He pulls out a small pink box from his pocket. It has a white ribbon with a small white bow. He hands it to Adaline, who takes it from his hands. She pulls the bow, and the ribbon falls off. She lifts off the box top and sees a beautiful gold necklace. Hanging from the necklace is a gold heart locket. On one side it is engraved with the words "I love you," and on the other side it has a small bird with a flower.

ADALINE. Oh, Oliver, it is wonderful!

She pulls the locket apart and sees a miniature painting of her and of Oliver together.

ADALINE. I'll wear it forever.

Oliver takes the necklace out of her hands, pulls it around her neck, and clasps it.

OLIVER. I better go. I love you, Adaline.

Adaline stands in the kitchen. She hears Oliver open the door, and he greets Aaron, who is already back from escorting the kids to school. Aaron looks over at Adaline and sees one hand on the new necklace and the other hand on her belly.

AARON, *to Adaline.* You feeling okay?

ADALINE. Yes, I've never felt better in my whole
    life!

The Next Day, October 13, 1860

The next day is just as nice as the day before. Oliver is arranging for the special picnic at the gazebo for their anniversary celebration. Two years of wedded bliss. Adaline is getting all dressed up, special hairdo, makeup, her best dress, and of course, her new necklace. She even sprays on some perfume. She places her new shoes on and starts to get up, but the shoes have a higher heel than she is used to and her left foot pulls to one side, making her shoe come off. She places it back on and walks down the stairs. She tells Aaron she is leavings and that he is in charge of the two little one. The other two are at school.

> ADALINE, *to Aaron.* Well, I'm off to meet my man
> for our special picnic!

> AARON. Enjoy yourself. Take all the time you
> want. I can take care of the little ones. They're
> safe with me.

Aaron starts looking around and realizes that he has already lost Jackson. Jackson has hidden himself under the kitchen sink.

> AARON, yelling. Jackson Leander Bixby, where are
> you? You come out right now!

Adaline opens and closes the front door and starts to walk out. She has gotten to the sidewalk and has started across the street when her ankle again wobbles and her shoe comes off.

> ADALINE, talking to herself out loud. For gosh
> sakes, at this rate I will be late!

She bends down to pick up the shoe so she can place it back on her foot. While she is stooping down, she does not even notice the wagon with two large horses turning the curve in back of her.

Aaron hears the scream and runs out of the front door. Looking around, he eventually sees down the street a wagon with horses. A gentleman is standing at the side of the wagon, the horses' reins in his hands.

> WAGON MASTER. Oh no! Oh no…

People along the sidewalks are running toward the scene. Aaron runs down the street and passes the wagon to see Adaline lying prone on the street. She has one shoe on and one shoe off.

Her blouse has dirt marks where horse hooves have made contact with her body. There is blood running out of her mouth and ears. The wagon owner is holding the reins of his horses to keep them from injuring her any further, but it is too late. The damage is done. Adaline is dead.

Aaron bends down and sits on the ground, grabbing Adaline's limp body into his. He starts to sob in disbelief. The sister that has always taken care of him is gone, and there is nothing he can do for her.

Oliver is still at the gazebo. He is wondering where Adaline is. He takes another look at the arrangement in front of him and grins with satisfaction. There is a large picnic basket on the table. Set out on special plates are cheeses and crackers, and wine has been poured into tall glasses. The napkins are there. He takes out his gold watch attached to his gold fob and pushes the button. The watch flips open, and he can see that it is past twelve noon. He then notices that people are running down the street that leads to his home. The adrenaline strikes him with a sense of foreboding. Adeline should have been here by now, he realizes, and his face starts to pale. He quickly gets up and starts to run down the street. Eventually, he can see a crowd in front of a wagon with two horses. As he approaches, he hears whispers.

> CROWD. It's him…let him through…oh, the
> poor man.

The crowd parts. He gets close enough to see Aaron on the ground with Adaline in his arms, crying. Aaron looks up to see Oliver standing over his shoulder. Oliver places his hand on Aaron's shoulder.

> OLIVER. I'll take over now.

Aaron gets up, and Oliver bends down to pick his wife up in his arms. He stands up with her limp body and walks back to his home with Aaron by his side.

OLIVER, *to Aaron.* Adaline just told me that we
were expecting our second child…

AARON. Oh my God!

As they enter the house, Jack is in the living room. He sees Oliver
with Adaline in his arms.

OLIVER, *to Aaron.* You'll need to watch Jack and
Walter. I'm going to take Adaline upstairs. I may
be up there for a while.

He starts to break down as he starts up the stairs, but slowly, one step
at a time, he makes it to the top and into their room. He closes the door.
Eventually, Aaron gets everyone together in the home, including
William, James, and even Benjamin. Aaron has reached out for Dr.
Smith, but not for Adaline, who he knows is dead, but for Oliver. Oliver
has not come out of the room for over a day.

DR. SMITH, *to Oliver, knocking on the bedroom
door.* Oliver, it's Dr. Smith. I need you to let
me in.

Oliver cracks open the door, wearing his clothing from the previous
day, which is now wrinkled.

DOCTOR. Let me in, Oliver. I'm here to help you.
I heard about Adaline. Don't you think it's time
to let the rest of the family grieve?

OLIVER, *reluctantly.* Come in.

He ever so slowly opens the door. The people downstairs can see
Adaline laid out on the bed before the door closes again behind the doctor.
The next day, Adaline is buried. Oliver takes William aside.

OLIVER, *to William*. I can't believe she is gone.
She had just told me we were expecting another
child. Life is going to be so different now. I can
let you and your brothers and sister stay in my
home for a while, but I just don't have the desire
to go back to work.

He takes his watch out to check the time. This time the watch fob
has a new item hanging from it, a heart-shaped locket.

OLIVER, *to William*. Adaline loved you a lot. She
knew how kind and gentle you are. That was
why she wanted you to be close to our home,
so she could be there if you ever needed her,
to protect you. I can sense that war is going to
start. I had talked to Adaline about joining the
Union forces, and she understood my path.

Oliver has no interest in his business or in the household after that
day. His little boy, Walter, reminds him so much of Adaline and of her
death that Walter would later go live with his grandmother Phebe Reed,
to be raised in her household.

Less than one month later, on November 15, 1860, in Lee County,
Iowa, James marries Henriette Marshall. It is hard to enjoy his wedding
after his sister's death, but life has to go on.

Chapter 6

The Civil War

As predicted, the Civil War begins soon after Abraham Lincoln is elected President. Iowa is a Union state fighting against the Confederate states. Benjamin, at eighteen, is the first to join the Civil War. On May 2, 1861, he joins the Sixth Infantry Regiment, Company H, of Iowa. Aaron, at twenty-one, is soon to follow; after all, he needs to protect his younger brother. He joins on July 12, 1861, into the same regiment and company as Benjamin. Then Oliver is next. He joins the Thirtieth Iowa Infantry at Keokuk, Iowa, and musters in for three years of federal service on September 20, 1862. James, twenty-five, is drafted on July 30, 1863, into the first congressional district of Iowa, but because he is married, he does not actually serve in combat.

Eventually, all the regiments and companies from Iowa come together in the Vicksburg Campaign. Each army knows what is at stake. Control of the Mississippi River would mean control of the supply lines by river. If the Union wins, it would split the Confederate states. Control of Vicksburg, Mississippi, would also allow a route to Atlanta, Georgia, one of the main targets to conquer, along with Richmond. Major General Grant and General Sherman have joined forces for control of the river and the land around it. In a major battle on June 17, 1863, at Black Creek Bridge, the Confederate forces under Pemberton are defeated and they flee across the river, burning bridges and boats to delay the Union Army from crossing. This allows Pemberton's forces to enter Vicksburg. After the Union forces reach an area outside of Vicksburg, they feel confident that they could bomb the city from the riverboats and artillery from land to force a quick surrender. But Vicksburg is well fortified, and they have the upper altitude. May 19 and May 22, the Union Army sends in a large number of soldiers to try to take Vicksburg. But Vicksburg is determined to repulse the Union forces. One Vicksburg resident, Mary Harwood, has a cannon in her front yard and is shooting it herself to keep the Union forces from climbing up the banks. There are an abnormally high number of casualties on the Union side.

Union Headquarters, Black Creek Bridge, Mississippi, May 21, 1863

Officer tents are set up. It is night, and planning is continuing for Major General Ulysses S. Grant and General William Tecumseh Sherman. There are lanterns hanging from the tentpoles, shedding light throughout. There is a table with a map.

> GRANT, to Sherman. We certainly got Pemberton
> on the run the other day at this spot on Black
> Creek Bridge. We defeated him and forced him
> to flee into Vicksburg. He only delayed us two
> days by burning the bridges and boats across
> the river. Now, all we have to do is to get him to
> surrender. He is stuck with no way out. We have
> the gunboats on the river, and the entire city is
> surrounded by our forces. I think if we send our
> troops up there tomorrow on May 22, we will
> be able to run through them into the city and
> take it. Our fight on the nineteenth was not as
> successful as I had hoped.

> SHERMAN. We will do something different this
> time. I will have the gunboats on the Mississippi
> River bombard the city of Vicksburg. You will

bombard Pemberton's troops from land. We'll
do this for three hours. Then we will send in our
troops, full force.

GRANT. Morale has been restored after our last
battle two days ago. The men have been well
nourished. We were able to forage for some
food supplies. Why, I saw a man last night
eating hardtack, and he pointed to me and said,
"Hardtack." Now everyone in camp is calling
me that.

SHERMAN. We have made ladders for the men to
use once they make it to the banks.

Grant is looking at a map that has items representing his regiments
and artillery. He starts to move some of these items around on the map.

GRANT. I'm going to order the Sixth Infantry
Regiment, Company H, Iowa, to head up
this bank here. The Thirtieth Infantry of Iowa
volunteers will head over to this bank here
with ladders to climb up the fortification. The
combination of our military forces should have
them surrendering by the end of tomorrow.

Vicksburg, Mississippi, May 22, 1863

Brigadier General John D. Stevenson advances well in two columns
against the redoubt. Included in his forces is the Thirtieth Infantry
Regiment of the Iowa volunteers, under Colonel William Torrence.
They had fought hard on May 19, when they were repulsed by the forces
at Vicksburg, but now, with good food in their bellies and a feeling of
victory, they march on up the banks to the fortified area of Vicksburg.
They hold ladders to help them scale the higher banks and eventually

reach the city. It is a hard walk, up rocky areas, and with shots from snipers on the hills above.

Oliver is among these men, struggling to get high enough to use their ladders to reach the city. You can see the exhaustion in his face, but also the hope that this one victory today will end the siege and that Vicksburg will surrender. There is sweat and dirt on his face and hands. Blisters are forming on his hands from holding on to the ladder, but he pushes onward, up the rocky hillside, and toward the bluff. He places his ladder and starts to climb. It is then that he sees the older woman standing behind her cannon, lighting the fuse.

> MARY HARWOOD, *screaming at the top of her lungs*. Take that, you damn Yankees! Go to hell! You'll never take our city!

> OLIVER, *jumping down and yelling*. Hit the deck, boys! There's a cannon up there!

The men dive to the ground as the cannonball hits the soil and explodes. Oliver could hear screams of agony. He could see the soil flowing upward and then feel a terrible pain in his right leg and right side.

When he awakens, he looks over and sees body parts lying around him. His fellow soldiers are dead. He could not get up, and as he tries to look down, he does not see his right leg. There is a large flow of blood coming out of his leg, so he takes his belt off and makes a tourniquet with a stick. Eventually, the medics find him.

> MEDIC. What's your name?

> OLIVER. Oliver Hazzard Perry Reed.

> MEDIC. That name sounds familiar. Hmmm…

> OLIVER. I was named after Oliver Hazard Perry, a US Navy officer in the War of 1812. He's the

one that said, "We have met the enemy, and they are ours."

MEDIC. How appropriate. Well, Oliver, it looks like you saved your own life today. That tourniquet stopped the bleeding that surely would have placed you into a grave. Let's see what we can do once we get you down this hill.

OLIVER. Sounds good to me. By all means, after you.

The medics take him down in a litter. He is given some emergency medical treatment. His leg is already gone from the knee down, and he has a wound to his side. He is waiting to be taken to Black Creek Bridge, where the injured are being held, when two familiar faces come up.

BENJAMIN, *to Oliver*. Why, look who is here! I didn't know we were fighting in the same battle.

AARON, *to Oliver*. You look badly injured. What happened?

OLIVER. You won't believe it, but a woman, Mary Harwood, had a cannon in her front yard. She shot out a cannonball that almost killed me. I lost my leg, and my side is injured. They are sending me to the back of the lines.

BEN, *to Oliver*. All this fighting for two days and many of us have died.

AARON. Grant asked Vicksburg if they wanted to surrender today, and they said no. So there you go! Who knows how long this is going to last now.

OLIVER. Well, if they were smart, the Army
should just hold back and let them starve.

AARON. I tell you what, Oliver, Ben and I are
going to finish this fight for you, so don't you
worry. I have a feeling we are going to be here
for a while.

They shake hands and say their farewells. As they are leaving, Oliver
is lifted up in his litter and is taken in the opposite direction.

Vicksburg, Mississippi, July 4, 1863

On July 4, 1863, Vicksburg surrenders. On a day that is a celebration
of our Declaration of Independence from England, Vicksburg will only
see the Fourth of July as a date of defeat at the hands of the Union
Army. Many of the residents, including Mary Harwood, will flee to
Texas as refugees.

Ben and Aaron go to see Oliver before they are sent off to the next
battle. Although in high spirits, Oliver does not look very well.

AARON. Hey, Oliver, as promised, we got that city
to surrender.

He and Ben give a little chuckle, and they are joined by Oliver.

AARON. I heard that most of the residents fled to
Texas, including that Harwood woman and her
family. Then General Grant took over her home
and made it into his new headquarters.

OLIVER. I hope they trash it and send that cannon
to the bottom of the Mississippi River.

BEN. When you get back home, will you say hello
to our family, let them know how we are doing?

OLIVER. Sure, I will. I just need to get some
strength. I want to see that son of mine.

BEN. While we were taking Vicksburg here in
Mississippi, there was another battle going
on at the same time. It was at Gettysburg, in
Pennsylvania, and we won there also. We must
really have those rebels worried. We should have
them surrendering anytime now.

AARON. Take care. We'll see you back in Iowa after
the war.

Black Creek Bridge, Mississippi,
Four Months Later, September 12, 1863

As time goes by, Oliver's wounds begin to fester and he gets fevers.
As he realizes that things are not going well, he decides to make out a
will. If he dies, he wants his watch, the only personal thing of value that
he owns, to be sent to his brother-in-law William Bixby. He is located
in a tent along with twenty-one other men. They are all in rows of cots.
He sees many of them carried out as they die. He knows he is going to
be next.

OLIVER, *to nurse.* Hey, nurse, come here. (*He
moans, coughs.*)

The nurse comes over and looks at the chart. She reads his name.

NURSE. Yes, Private Reed, what can I do for you?

OLIVER. I want to write a letter, a will. If I die,
I want my watch to go to my brother-in-law
William Bixby, in Montrose, Iowa. Can you
help me?

NURSE. Yes, I help all the young men here at this
tent. What do you want it to say?

He begins his letter and gives her instructions on what to do if he dies. And on September 22, 1863, four months to the day he was injured, Oliver dies of his wounds at Black Creek Bridge, Mississippi. Eventually, his body is laid to rest at the Vicksburg National Cemetery. Due to the hardships and confusion of war, information about his death, his letter, and his package are lost for almost a year.

Montrose, Iowa, September 1864

A package with a letter is sent to William Bixby in Montrose, Iowa. It has initially gotten lost and has recently been found. It takes almost a year to get to him. William has never had a package sent to him before, and he has to pick it up at the railway station. He does not know what to expect.

WILLIAM, to telegraph operator. Excuse me, sir, I
believe there is a package for me to pick up. My
name is William Bixby.

OPERATOR. Yes, William Bixby, I have it right
here.

He ruffles through some items in a bin and pulls out the small package. He hands it to William.

WILLIAM. Thank you very much.

William goes to the side of the station and sits on a bench. He cuts the string that is holding the package together with a pocketknife from his pants pocket and finds the letter.

9/12/1863

Dear William:

If you have gotten this package, it means that I am dead. I was wounded badly in the Battle of Vicksburg. My right leg was blown off by a cannon. At first, it looked like I was going to be all right, but infections have taken hold and I have had several fevers.

I saw your brothers Aaron and Benjamin. They were here at the same battle. After Vicksburg was taken, I heard that they headed toward Atlanta, Georgia, with Sherman's Army.

Your sister talked about you all the time to me. She told me about your kind and gentle ways. I hope you can stay that way, even in this time of war and violence.

The package holds the only item I have left in this world of value. It is my gold watch and gold watch fob. You will notice that it still has attached the locket that I gave to my sweet Adaline, your sister. I want my body to be placed next to hers in the cemetery where she lies. I will be with her in heaven.

With many thoughts your way and to all my family,

O. H. P. Reed

William's eyes are shedding tears at the thought of Oliver and his sister Mary. They loved each other so much, and it ended in tragedy. Walter is now an orphan. It only brings back memories of his parents dying so close together just four years earlier. He became an orphan at fourteen. He opens the box and pulls out the watch. He handles it gently in his hands, inspecting the artwork. He opens the locket and sees the miniature painting of Oliver and Adaline. He has been concentrating so hard on the letter and the box that he has not noticed, until now, the great commotion coming from the railway station. The telegraph operator is posting a notice up. He is hammering a small nail into a piece of white paper. It is a listing of the war dead from Iowa. As William gets up, he connects the watch fob to his shirt and places the watch into his pants pocket. He folds the letter up and puts it into his shirt pocket. He could hear screams and moans as a woman recognizes the name of her son.

>OLDER WOMAN. No, not my Henry! Dear God,
> why Henry?

She sobs, and a young man, probably her son, helps her walk back to her home.

>YOUNG BOY. There's Uncle Robert's name!

The young boy starts to run from the board, probably to tell his family that a name they know is in the list. William strains a little to see over some hats and heads. He sees a name he already knew would be there, Oliver Hazzard Perry Reed. And then he sees a name he was not expecting: Benjamin Bixby, June 27, 1864, Little Kennesaw Mountain, Georgia. The shock is almost overwhelming, and he feels faint. His brother is dead. He looks harder to see if Aaron's name is there, but it's not. He suddenly feels a hand on his shoulder. It is Alonzo Crandel, the neighbor that had taken him in when his parents died.

>MR. CRANDEL, *s.* I see some names there that
> are your family. I'm sorry, William. I remember
> your brother Benjamin. He was a nice boy.

>WILLIAM. I don't see Aaron's name on the board.
> They were together, in the same regiment and
> company. I hope that means he is still alive.

>MR. CRANDEL. You know, my son John enlisted
> about a year ago. That's why I come here when
> they post names. So far, we have been lucky. His
> name has not shown up. Does the Reed family
> know about Oliver?

WILLIAM. No. I will go to Phebe's home. She
has been taking care of Walter for Oliver after
he enlisted. I feel badly for Walter, being an
orphan.

MR. CRANDEL. Brings back a lot of memories.
My thoughts are with you and your family. Let
me know if I can be of help.

WILLIAM. Thank you, Mr. Crandel. You have
always been there for my family.

MR. CRANDEL. Well, I knew your parents. They
were good people, like you. That was why we
took you in. We knew we could trust you.

William does not look forward to giving the news to his brothers
and sister. Not one, but two names. They've always known death as a
possibility when enlisting into the infantry. He drops by Phebe Reed's
home first. He knocks on their door. Phebe answers.

PHEBE. Hi, William! You here to visit with Walter?
He always loves to see you and play with you in
the afternoon.

WILLIAM. I'm sorry, Phebe. I'm not here to play
with Walter. I just came from the telegraph
office. They posted a new listing of the war
dead…

Phebe senses what is coming. It is a family's nightmare.

PHEBE. It's Oliver, isn't it? I was so afraid this
would happen. My sweet boy! Oh my God,
poor Walter.

She looks over at Walter, who has started to toddle up, not knowing that he is now an orphan.

PHEBE. Where did it happen?

WILLIAM. He was at the Battle of Vicksburg,
        Mississippi, in 1863 when he got his wounds,
        but he did not die until four months later from
        infection. I'm not sure why it took so long for
        them to get the news to us. Before he died, he
        made up a letter for me and sent me a package.
        I just got the package today. Here, you can read
        the letter.

He pulls the letter from his pocket and hands it to Phebe. She takes it, opens it, pulls her glasses up to her eyes, and reads it.

PHEBE. It was a slow and painful death. I almost
        wish he had died quickly in battle.

Tears are running down her cheek. She looks down and sees the watch that William now wears.

PHEBE. I am glad he had a chance to decide who
        would get his watch.

WILLIAM. I'm afraid there was another name,
        Benjamin Bixby.

PHEBE. Wasn't he your youngest brother to go to
        war? Such a waste! War is terrible. It takes all the
        good men.

WILLIAM. I have to go talk with my sister and
        brothers. It is a hard task.

He lowers his head as he walks down her porch to the street. He makes the long walk a little longer until he reaches the house. He opens the door, and Lewis, Elizabeth, and Jackson come up to give him a hug. James and his wife are also there.

> WILLIAM. I have some bad news. I just came from
> the telegraph office.

There are gasps, as they all know that any minute now their world is going to change forever. A family member is gone.

> WILLIAM. Oliver's name was there. He died
> from wounds that he received in the Vicksburg
> Campaign.

> ELIZABETH. Oh, poor Walter! Now he is an
> orphan, like we are.

> WILLIAM, *his voice shaking*. There was another
> name. It's…it's Benjamin.

There are screams of horror and sadness, and tears well up in the eyes of Henriette, the wife of James.

> HENRIETTE. James, your brother…I can't
> believe it.

> JAMES. Damn this war! It's not going to be happy
> until all the young men in the nation are killed
> and buried.

He walks out of the room and out the front door. Henriette follows. Elizabeth, Lewis, and Jackson hug William. Not only have they lost a brother, but they've also lost their uncle, the owner of their home. Just as they thought, their life would never be the same.

Montrose, Iowa, September 1865

Aaron returns home after his second enlistment is over, on July 21, 1865. President Abraham Lincoln had been assassinated in April, and President Johnson is now in charge. Aaron is discharged as a full corporal in Louisville, Kentucky. It is a great homecoming, and the family comes together to hear Aaron's stories of the war. They are in the kitchen, sitting in the chairs around the table.

> AARON, *to family*. Well, as you all know, Ben and
> I joined the Sixth Infantry Regiment, Company
> H, Iowa. This meant that we saw the same
> battles. One of the most exciting was the Battle
> of Vicksburg. We were part of the surrender on
> July 4, 1863. It was there that we saw Oliver
> after he had been wounded. His leg had been
> blown off, and he had other wounds to his side.
> When we left him, he was weak but seemed to
> be doing well at Black Creek Bridge. But I have
> since learned, as you all have, that Oliver died of
> his wounds four months later. What a loss! He
> was a great man. Our regiment joined Sherman's
> Army in the Atlanta Campaign. We hit several
> battles at Resaca, Hope Church, and Big
> Shana. We then came to the Little Kennesaw
> Mountain in Georgia. Sherman wanted us to
> take the top of the mountain, but it already had
> the Confederate Army on top. We had to push
> artillery up the hillside.

Battlefield at Little Kennesaw Mountain, June 27, 1864

> BEN, *to Aaron*. This is crazy! Why would Sherman
> want us to take a hillside that is already full of
> rebels? And pushing these artillery cannons up

with us. I feel like a goddamn mule. Forget "my
kingdom for a horse." I'd give everything I own
for a really strong mule!

AARON. Too bad the rebs killed them all. Besides,
mules can't take gunfire and artillery, only
horses can.

Gunfire and cannons are exploding all around them. Men are falling,
screaming in agony. It is hell.

AARON. If we can take this hill, we can set up our
own cannons and the rebels will be running all
the way to Atlanta! You can do it, Ben. We have
been through much worse than this.

BEN. Okay, let's push together. One…two… three!

The cannon dislodges from some debris and starts to move uphill.
Aaron also notices that their commanding officer has just been shot and
is probably deceased.

AARON. Well, it looks like we're not the only ones
being used as fodder for Sherman's Army. There
goes the last of our officers. It's up to us to get
this job done now, with or without the orders.

You can hear them breathing harder and harder, grunting as they
push the cannon farther and farther up the hillside. And then it happens:
a bullet hits Benjamin square in the middle of his forehead. Blood starts
to ooze out, and he starts to fall, a last groan issuing out of his mouth.
Aaron grabs him as he falls. His death is as instant as they come, but
Aaron's agony is just beginning as he holds his limp brother in his arms.

AARON. Goodbye, dear brother.

He looks up from his dead brother to the top of the hill. His only desire right now is to kill all the rebels on that hill and to get his cannon on top. He lays Ben's body down and grabs a lone Union soldier running up the hill. He is a very husky man with good muscles, perfect for the task.

> AARON. You need to help me push this cannon up
> the hill. We need it to make the rebels run and
> end this fighting. Are you with me?

> SOLDIER. You bet! Let's do it.

They both push the cannon, and eventually the other soldiers in his regiment have either killed or dislodged the remaining rebels from the hill. They set up the cannon, and the others with ammunition are not far behind. They begin to load and fire it at the forces below. It gets the results they want. The rebels are running the other way.

> SOLDIER. I saw you coming up the hill when the
> other soldier was shot next to you. I saw you
> hold him. Did you know him well?

Aaron looks down, agony on his face.

> AARON. Yes. He was my brother, Ben.

> SOLDIER. Well, I don't think we could have gotten
> this cannon up without your courage, and now
> look, we have control over the entire battlefield.
> The rebels are running, just as you said.

There is a grin of relief on his face as he looks at Aaron.

> AARON. Ben and I re-enlisted in January so we
> could see the end to this war. Now it looks like
> I will be the only one left to see that. What is
> your name?

SOLDIER. It is John, John Crandel.

AARON, looking at him in disbelief. Is your father's
    name Alonzo?

JOHN. Yes. How did you know?

AARON. Your family took in my brother William,
    William Bixby, when we all became orphans.
    I'm so glad to meet you.

He gives a handshake, and then a manly hug.

JOHN. Dang, you never know who you are going
    to meet next in this war.

The two of them would become partners in the remainder of Aaron's
enlistment. They watch each other's back, and both survive to come home.
Eventually, the fighting for the day comes to an end, and the wounded
and dead are being taken care of on the battlefield. Aaron drops down
the mountain, taking the path he had come with the cannon. He finds
the body of his brother, picks him up, and carries him to the bottom of
the hillside. They are already digging graves for the men who have fallen.
This will be a temporary place, until a more suitable grave site can be
created. But for now, it is the best they can do. As Ben's body is laid into
the grave, Aaron makes sure that there is a pole placed at the head of
the grave with his name, regiment, and company etched into the wood.

AARON. Goodbye, Ben. You did good. You were
    brave till the end. Like Adaline before you, I
    held your limp dead body in my arms. She tried
    to protect us, and I tried to protect you, but to
    no avail.

In Montrose, Iowa, Aaron is telling the story to his family.

AARON, *to family*. It was a tough day. One you can never forget. But your brother was brave, and we can all be proud of him. We took that hill in his name and with the help of our fellow Iowans. I later heard that Ben was laid to rest in the Marietta National Cemetery in Marietta, Georgia.

WILLIAM. I hear that Oliver was buried at the National Cemetery in Vicksburg, Mississippi. I know he wanted to be buried next to our sister Adaline. He wanted to be next to his sweet Adaline.

William starts to grab his watch fob.

WILLIAM, *to Aaron*. How is it that you came back as a corporal?

AARON. Well, after the Battle of Little Kennesaw Mountain, word got around that even after our commanders were all down, I encouraged our men to take the hill, which turned the battle around. I guess it was a reward that they promoted me to full corporal a few weeks before my enlistment was over on July 21, 1865. They left me at Louisville, Kentucky, when my enlistment ended. Believe me, Louisville is a long way from here. It would have been a lot harder getting back, but they sold me one of their war horses that they didn't need anymore. I've named him Travis after Robert E. Lee's horse.

JAMES. Well, we're glad you're back home, Aaron.

William kind of nudges Aaron on the arm.

> WILLIAM, *whispering to Aaron.* Can I talk to you
> for a moment?

> AARON. Sure.

They get up and walk outside.

> WILLIAM. You know, when all this war stuff
> started, I was too young, and then when I was
> old enough, I was the only one old enough
> to take care of our younger brothers and
> sister. Things here at Montrose have been very
> depressed, and it has been hard to get any work
> at all. It seems like the only place you can go
> nowadays is into the Army.

> AARON. Well, even that is thinning out now that
> the Civil War is coming to an end. But I can tell
> you where the next area will be. It's a hot keg
> waiting to burst. It is out where the Indians are.

He looks at William and puts his hand on his shoulder.

> AARON. It's time for you to go. James and I can
> take care of everything here. Start looking at
> your options with the Army, and when it comes,
> let us know.

> WILLIAM. Thanks, Aaron. I understand that for
> volunteering in the Army, you get a parcel of
> land. Are you going to take it or sell it outright?

> AARON. I haven't decided. I have to see where it
> is. It certainly is a perk, if you can survive, to

have a piece of land you can call your own. You
can also get homesteads along the railway tracks
for a minimal amount, but you have to stay on
it and improve it for five years. The path that
you take, William, will be up to you now, but
remember what Ma and Pa said: 'Your future is
to the West.'

Aaron grins at William. He has acknowledged that William is now
a man ready to start his own life and to make his own decisions and
that his family will support what those are.

Chapter 7

Back to Sheridan, Wyoming, 1918

It has been quite a while since Ed joined Ben outside of the substitute hospital. All of a sudden, they see and hear the man they saw earlier, Sam. He was the man who had the young boy in his arms. He is staggering down the stairs of the building, in grief and agony. The doctor is at the double doors.

> DOCTOR. I'm sorry, Sam. It was all we could
> do. His fever was so high, and then he got
> pneumonia.

> SAM He was all I had. You're a quack! I'm going to
> make sure that everyone hears what a quack you
> really are!

The anger is making him sick, and he almost loses his balance. He grabs the railing, bends over, and breathes hard. The doctor starts to come down the stairs, but Sam throws him an angry look back at him.

> SAM. You stay away from me! First, my wife... and
> now my Charlie...

He makes his way off the stairs and walks in anger until he is out of sight.

ED, *to Ben.* Come on, Ben, it's been a while since
we saw Dad. Let's go back in.

They walk across the lawn, now green, with only small areas where snow is still present. They pass by the doctor, and they can see how affected he is by the loss of a child and the insults of the father. He has been working straight for two days now, with only a few hours of rest. The look on his face shows that he is questioning his abilities to be a doctor. He really doesn't know what he is facing. He doesn't know how to treat it. And it seems like whatever he does makes no difference. At this point, he doesn't have the strength to give his bereaved families any emotional help. He hasn't told anyone this, but his own grandfather was in the hospital and just died today. As Ed and Ben pass by, the doctor has taken his glasses off and is trying to clean them with a handkerchief. They get to their family group and look down at their father in the hospital cot. He seems better now and is sleeping.

ED, *to Mom.* Hey, Mom, looks like Dad is doing
okay.

MOM. The doctor gave him some of that new
medication, aspirin. It seems to have lowered his
temperature. He is not sweating as much.

SISTER. And look, he is finally sleeping!

ED, *to Mom.* Do you want a break? I would like to
take you to the wagon outside. The weather is
much better. It is warm and sunny. It might do
you some good to get away. The sisters are here,
and Ben too.

Jessie looks worried but gets up, leaving the blanket behind in a neat, folded pile.

She takes Ed's arm, and he escorts her through the double door. She is sixty-five years old, about five feet two, a little rotund, with a simple plaid dress on. Her hands show the arthritis in them. Her hair is black with gray mixed in; it is parted down the middle, and each side has a long braid of hair. Leather straps hold the braids, with a few beads dangling at the ends. Her face is dark and shows the many years spent in the sun and the harsh conditions she has endured. There is a small scar on her neck. Her eyes are brown, and they squint a lot. She should be wearing glasses. The doctor is still leaning against the doorjamb as they approach the double doors.

> JESSIE, *to the doctor.* Thank you, Doctor, for all you
> are doing for the sick. I know it is a tough job,
> and we really appreciate it.

The doctor gives a smile, the first one he has been able to muster for a long time.

> JESSIE, *to the doctor.* Are you doing okay? It looks
> like you could use a little rest. Is your family
> among the patients?

The doctor is surprised by her question, as no one has cared about him or his family during all this, not even his fellow assistants.

> DOCTOR. Yes, my grandfather was in the hospital.

> JESSIE. How is he doing?

> DOCTOR. He didn't make it.

> JESSIE. I'm so sorry to hear that. From the way
> things look, I think everyone in the world is
> going to lose a family member.

> ED, *to Mom.* Wow, Mom, that sounds bad.
> Hopefully, it will stop before that.

THE DOCTOR, *to Ed.* I'm afraid she might be
right.

The doctor gets some more strength and walks back into the building
Ed and Jessie continue to walk down to their wagon. Ed gives the horses
some water, then attaches food bags with some grain.

ED, *to Mom.* Can you tell me what it was like in the
early days, before you met Dad?

JESSIE. You've heard these stories before, but if you
really want me to tell you again, I can do this. It
will take my mind off your dad.

ED. Please, Mom.

JESSIE. Okay.

JESSIE begins her story.

JESSIE. We are a member of the Northern
Cheyenne Indian Tribe. My great-great grandma
was Warpath Woman. Her husband was
Bearman. They had my great grandma Twin
Woman, also called Buffalo Appearing Woman,
or in our language, Hestâhkêha'e. She had my
grandmother, Humpback Woman, also called
Lightning Stands, Josie, or in our language,
Whog-coo-tos. She lived a long time, and I
knew her well. We were close. She had several
husbands. With High Back Wolf, a Peace Chief
of the Southern Cheyenne, she had my aunt
Aurora, also known as Snake Woman, or in our
language Sish-sa-no-vo-he-a. She lived a long
time, and I met her. Having the same father, she
was a half-sister to the Peace Chief Black Kettle.

Another daughter, my mother, was Minihe,
also known as Shell Woman, and my father was
Lakota, called Sioux by the White man, by the
name of Chasaway. I was born around 1853 in
an area that may now be Nebraska or Wyoming.
Things have changed so much I can't tell you
now. My mother had another husband, Henry
Rouleau, a French-Canadian fur trader. He may
have been the father of my half-sister, Sallie, also
called Spotted Tail, or in our language, Woostaa.
She had a nickname, Vehiogaha, or Little White
Girl. She was born around September 1850.
She had a daughter with Captain James Cahill
of the Second Cavalry at Fort D. A. Russell,
Wyoming. He was a veteran of the War between
the States. Her name was Lucy, also known
as Vino Museae. Sallie then married George
Harris, a Private from the US Cavalry and later
an innkeeper and cattle rancher. It was because
of George that I met your father, William Bixby.
From my early years, I and my tribe have been
affected by the White man. My early years have
bad memories of what the White man is capable
of, but my later years have shown me the good
that White men can accomplish if they want to.

She looks at Ed, and her face has anguish on it.

JESSIE. You have felt the brunt of the White man's
impact. Your Indian side against the White
man side, and your White man side against
your Indian side. These two sides have been in
conflict for so long I wonder if they can ever
be reconciled. I wonder if you can ever place

your two halves together to find peace within
yourself.

ED. Mankind can do terrible things to his fellow
man. When humans start naming you as a
"savage" or a "heathen," then they are trying to
make you less than a man, and this gives them
the license to treat you like an animal or a slave,
and then they don't feel so bad when they kill
you. No matter who said it, that "the only good
Indian is a dead Indian," it certainly expressed
the White man's desire to eradicate all the
Indian tribes. Tell me more, Mom, about the
battle.

JESSIE. Before I was born, our tribe signed the
Fort Laramie Treaty in 1851. This treaty gave
us lands that included parts of Nebraska,
Wyoming, and Colorado. After gold was found
in the Rocky Mountains, the White man was
mining for this, but they also started to settle
in our land. By 1861 we were starting to fight
for our lands again. In February 8, 1861, Black
Kettle signed a new treaty, which gave us less
land, six hundred square miles, but gave us an
annuity each year. This was the Treaty of Fort
Wise. However, not all our bands agreed with
this treaty, and they continued to cause raids
and harm against the White man. In 1864,
Black Kettle went to Fort Lyon to seek safety
for our people. He was sent to Sand Creek,
Colorado Territory, so that our men could hunt,
and this is the first battle I remember.

Sand Creek, Colorado Territory
Thanksgiving Day, November 29, 1864

President Lincoln, in 1862, restored during the Civil War the celebration of Thanksgiving Day to be the fourth Thursday in November. November 29, 1864, is Thanksgiving for the year.

About sixty-four tepees are set up in a circle, each with their flap openings facing east, toward the rising of the sun. There is a large meadow by Sand Creek. Among these tepees is that of Black Kettle, which has a US flag outside on a lodgepole. He has been told that this will guarantee safety to his tribe by Fort Lyon. There are a few horses in a corral, but most are gone as many of the men have left to hunt for food. Racks are outside, with hides drying for leather.

> JOSIE, *to her daughter Minihie.* As an elder, I was
> allowed to attend the meeting with the Chiefs
> at Fort Lyon. We have been given this safe place
> along Sand Creek to set up our tepees in peace.

> MINIHIE. I do not feel comfortable about this.
> The White man has never been able to keep
> their promises about land or our safety.

> JOSIES. The Big Chief of the Territory of
> Colorado, John Evans, has guaranteed our tribe
> a safe place to be. They have also made friends
> with Chief Black Kettle. He is determined to
> keep peace among our people. I have seen so
> many of our people die in battle. I want to have
> hope that this will work.

In come Sallie and Jessie from playing outside. Sallie is fourteen, and Jessie is eleven. A little puppy is running with them. Most of the warriors have left to hunt for food, and everyone is hoping that they find plenty for all.

MINIHIE, *to her children*. You are old enough to
be doing more than playing with a puppy. You
need to go collect some more water. Yesterday's
water is dead. We need the new alive water for
today. Now, go get some.

She hands them a wooden bucket. The girls leave quickly, with the
puppy.

They reach the water's edge. It is cold. You would have to run quite
a way to get to the other edge, and it is deep in places. You would have
to know how to swim. But they have never learned how. Some women
are washing clothes. Some young boys are throwing rocks into the creek.
They are challenging one another to see who can throw the farthest.
Sallie goes over.

SALLIE, *to boys*. I can throw farther than that.

She picks up a rock and hurls it. It arches upward and makes it all
the way to the other side. It's about twice as far as the boys had been
able to throw.

ONE BOY. Wow, Sallie, you would make a good
warrior!

They giggle and run away before Sallie can grab them.

Jessie has already placed the bucket in the cold water and has filled it
up by the time Sallie returns. Sallie and Jessie walk back with the bucket,
each holding a half of the handle, slopping a little each step they take.
The puppy is trying to nip at their feet.

SALLIE, *to Jessie*. Jeez, Jessie, you filled the bucket
too full. My moccasins are getting wet!

They approach the tepee and enter.

MINIHIE. Well, it is about time. Go place the
    bucket over there.

All of a sudden, they can feel the ground under them start to vibrate.

MINIHIE. Is it buffalo I hear headed for our camp?

And then there are sounds of men on horses. Josie knows what this means immediately and sounds the alarm for her family as she grabs two knives. After she rises, she places them into her belt.

JOSIE. Hurry, out of the tepee! Run as fast as you
    can to the river! We need to head upstream as
    quickly as we can.

She grabs her grandchildren's hands and runs with her daughter out of the tepee entrance. As they exit the flap, they can see gun smoke is thick near the outer rim of tepees. Screaming can be heard as women are hit by bullets and they fall. Black Kettle has also gone to the front of his tepee and is waving a white flag and standing next to the American flag. His family members are huddled with him. But the armed men on horseback are not stopping.

Josie and her family are now headed to the water's edge, where Jessie and Sallie had been just minutes before. They hear the yelp of the puppy as it is injured. Jessie looks back and sees others trying to escape the way they are escaping, but many are falling. Some of the warriors still in camp are now shooting their guns, and others have arrows. She can see a few of the uniformed men falling from their horses. The young boys that they had seen earlier are already dead, face down in the dirt.

Now they are in the cold water, trying to walk up the creek. It is so cold Jessie can't feel her feet, causing her to lose her footing. She starts to flow away from her family, into the deeper part of the creek, and she does not know how to swim. Her leather dress, now soaked with water, pulls her down. Jessie starts to panic.

JESSIE. Grama, Mama, help me!

JOSIE. Oh my gosh, Minihie, Jessie is going to
     drown!

Josie sloshes back downstream and grabs Jessie before she goes down
for the second time. As she does, they can see Black Kettle trying to get
across the creek with his wife, Medicine Woman Later. She is shot in
the back, and he helps her make it across the waters. But he can't stay,
or he, too, will be shot; he has to leave her and runs upstream. Jessie
can see that more shots are hitting Medicine Woman Later. Jessie feels
a sting against her throat. Josie gets Jessie into shallower water, and they
start catching up with Sallie.

Again, Jessie can see the fighting from the banks. Some of the men
have dismounted and are killing women point-blank. One has a child in
her arms, and it is grabbed from her arms and dashed against a leather
rack. Its skull shatters. The woman is dragged by the hair, is mounted,
and then shot. They can see that smoke is in the air, as the uniformed
men have set the village on fire. The screaming does not seem to stop.
As they get past the encampment, Josie slows them down. The bank is
high here, on the same side as where the tepees had been.

JOSIE. Here, we stop here and start to dig. Come
     on, dig like your life depends on it, because it
     does!

She takes the knives out and gives one to Minihie. They can dig
faster, and the children pull large pieces of bank away and throw it into
the creek. They start to hear horses above them. They are snorting.

There are about two of them. Josie has everyone stand quietly against
the embankment, her arm against her grandchildren, pressing them
further against the wall. She puts her finger to her mouth, a gesture to
keep them quiet. The uniformed men on horseback start to shoot at
others who can be seen still trying to get upstream. As the victims fall,
their blood taints the creek with red and flows by Josie's family. When

the horses disappear, she has them dig again. Finally, there is enough room dug into the bank for all four of them to creep into. They will be wet and cold for a very long time.

They continue to hear the noises above. Begging for mercy has no effect, and they can hear shots ring out soon afterward. Horses are now being taken across the creek and up the creek and down the creek. They do not see Josie or her family. The hardest thing for them to hear was the laughter from the murders as they bragged about their accomplishments.

> PRIVATE 1, *to Private 2.* Did you see how I shot
> that brave right through the heart? He dropped
> like a big buffalo. Boom!

> PRIVATE 2. I got three of the little ones all crying
> for mama. That's payback for the Burns Ranch,
> where all the homesteaders were scalped.

> PRIVATE 1. Well, the Colonel says that they all die,
> no prisoners, so let's get with it. I think I see two
> hiding in the bushes across the creek. Let's go!

They pull their horses through the stream and rush across to get what turns out to be two women hiding in the bush. As they run out, trying to escape, shots can be heard as they are killed.

Upstream and on the other side of the bank, they can see Black Kettle and a whole group of young men, women, and children. Many of them are his close family members. They have set up an area of safety using the sand from the banks and have several soldiers shooting at them. They have a few guns, and Black Kettle is helping to reload them. Suddenly, they can see several men trying to get to the embankment, running down the creek. Most of them are shot before they can reach the embankment, but one will be successful.

JOSIE, *in a hushed voice, to Minihie.* Look, it is
    George Bent, the son of the Indian trader
    William Bent and Owl Woman!

As he reaches the embankment and is jumping over, he is shot in the hip. Black Kettle helps him into their enclosure.

They can hear two soldiers on the opposite bank, above the creek, and two soldiers on the same side they are betting how many women and children they can pick off from the far bank above. They can see occasionally a woman or child fall as they are shot down.

PRIVATE 3. I bet you $1 that I can get that little
    boy with the feather in his hair.

PRIVATE 4. Okay.

Bang! THE boy goes down.

PRIVATE 3. See, I told you I could shoot good!

PRIVATE 4. Here you go.

HE HANDS over the $1.

PRIVATE 4. Now, I want to see if I can get that
    young squaw. How much you willing to bet?

PRIVATE 3. How about $2?

Bang! But the young Indian is still standing, the shot hitting the embankment instead.

PRIVATE 4. Dang.

PRIVATE 3. Hah!

Finally, the sun is ready to set and darkness will be approaching. It is only then that the uniformed soldiers begin to huddle back at the Indian camp. Their shooting has finally stopped.

> UNIFORMED MAN. Colonel, sir, all the Indians that we could find have been killed as ordered. We even made sure that the wounded would not survive. There are no prisoners.

> COLONEL JOHN M. CHIVINGTON. Good job, Officer. You know what they say, "The only good Indian is a dead Indian." We must kill all the Indians, including the women and children, for "the nits produce the louse." Let's leave a real message to these savages. I want you to mutilate the bodies. I want you to take trophies back home. Let the people of Denver know that we are here to protect them from these heathens!

> CAPTAIN SILAS SOULE. Colonel, this is wrong. I have stated from the beginning of this campaign that we have no right to kill these people, and I have refused to do so. This was a peaceful tribe, and they had only weapons for hunting game.

> COLONEL. You are a coward, and I will be filing court-martial papers against you for disobeying orders. Not only did you not shoot as ordered, but I also hear that you actually let some of the Indians on horseback go right through your ranks, allowing them to escape. This is inexcusable!

His face is turning red, and spit is starting to come out of his mouth.

He is so angry even his horse is becoming frightened and is starting to move back and forth.

> CAPTAIN. I am not afraid of you, Colonel. Your
> high aspirations for political power are over.
> Once people hear what really happened here
> today, of the lack of compassion and brutality,
> you will be the one court-martialed!

> COLONEL. Get out of my sight! You are a coward,
> an Indian hugger! Go back to Fort Lyon, and I
> will finish what needs to be done here. I'll take
> care of you later.

He pulls on his reins and leaves the side of Captain Soule. The Captain and his regiment head back to Fort Lyon.

As ordered, the fetuses from women are cut out of their stomach. Thighs are cut open. Others have their intestines dragged out of their body. Their eyes are poked out, fingers cut off for their jewelry, ears and noses cut off, and many are scalped. The genitals of men are cut off, and their testicles will be made into bags to hold tobacco. The women's breasts and genitalia are cut off and used around the horn on their saddles. It seems like they would never leave. And when they do, the members of the village that have survived come back to see the horror.

Black Kettle walks down the river to find the bank where he had left his dear wife. She had been shot many times but had not been mutilated like many of the others. He walks up to her and lovingly starts to pick her up to bury her, but then he hears a moan. She is still alive. The cold river has frozen many of her wounds so that she has not bled to death. But her injuries are many and very severe.

> BLACK KETTLE, *to wife*. My dear, sweet wife. I
> am so glad to see that you still live! Let me pick
> you up and carry you to our camp. We need to
> see what has happened there.

MEDICINE WOMAN LATER Why did they do
    this? We were peaceful and friendly. We have
    been betrayed. We have been murdered!

BLACK KETTLE. I know something very wrong
    has happened. I can't believe that our friends at
    Fort Lyon had anything to do with this.

He slowly lifts his wife and carries her on his shoulders to the other
side of the river to what is left of the camp. He has to avoid bodies that
are floating and bobbing in the creek.

Slowly the survivors come back. They wail with grief, and they wail
with anger. As they pick up the bodies of their family to bury, there is
a surprise. Under the body of her dead mother, an infant is still alive.
It is a miracle and one of the things that would be remembered and
carried down by the descendants of Humpback Woman for generations.

YOUNG INDIAN WOMAN. Here, give me the
    baby. I lost my infant today. I will adopt this
    one and raise it as my own.

The village is in total desolation. Everything has been burned. There
are no buffalo robes to put on and no food for the winter. As Josie's
family shivers on the riverbank, Josie sees something.

JOSIE, *to Jessie*. Let me look at your neck.

She pulls Jessie close to her and examines her neck with concern.

JOSIE. You were shot, Jessie, probably as you were
    in the deep water! It is a small wound, but it
    will probably leave a scar. It will be forever a
    memory of this day and this tragedy.

JESSIE. Why, Grandma? Why did the uniformed
    men come down the hill and kill us?

JOSIE. They do not want to share the land with us.

JESSIE. But there is so much land, Grandma. Have
we not signed treaties to share the land?

JOSIE. They will not be happy until all of us are
dead and all the land is theirs.

BLACK KETTLE, *to the survivors.* I have decided
that we need to start traveling to Big Timbers
at Smokey Hill River, where the Dog Soldiers
have their camp. It will be a journey of several
days, with many injured members. But this is
the closest camp near our location, and we will
be safe there.

INDIAN BRAVE. What gives you the right to
be Chief among us? You are a Suthai, not a
Cheyenne! We cannot trust you. You told us
that this camp would be safe, and look at what
happened! You are no longer fit to be our leader.

JOSIE. Black Kettle was assured by the White man
that we would be safe. He has been honest in his
dealings with the White man, but they have not
been with him.

GEORGE BENT. Black Kettle is right. The closest
camp is the Dog Soldiers. We need to seek
them out.

Black Kettle places his wife on his own shoulders, and they walk
slowly along the coure of the river. George has to use a large stick he
has found to walk, and it is slow and full of pain with every step. They
spend the night sleeping in the cold, with little warmth and no food.
Those that are not severely injured gather short grass with their hands

to make small fires for warmth. Others gather long grass to lay on the injured, who huddle together for warmth.

MINIHIE, a medicine woman, to George Bent.
Here, let me look at your wound.

She looks at the back of his thigh. He wenches in pain.

MINIHIE. You have been shot in the back of the
thigh, and it has gone through the front. No
bone has been hit. You are lucky. Here is some
medicine for the wound. You will need to be
watchful for infection. You should go and be
with your father, William, for a while, so you
can heal.

She grinds in her hand some herbs, moistens them, and lays them into the wound. She then puts some cloth over them.
She then goes over to Medicine Woman Later.

MINIHIE, *to Black Kettle.* She is badly injured. She
has been shot nine times. You will need to care
for her for many months. It is going to be a slow
process for her to recover.

BLACK KETTLE. She has been a good wife. I will
do whatever is needed to ensure that she will
survive.

He bends over and kisses her tenderly on the cheek.
The next morning, they are surprised and happy to see a string of Indian ponies and Cheyenne with supplies appearing in the horizon.

INDIAN ON HORSEBACK. Black Kettle, we
heard about the attack on your village. Some
men in your tribe escaped your camp by

jumping up on some ponies that got away from the corral. Apparently, there was a Captain with his regiment that did not shoot at them and allowed them to escape. They rode all night and reached the Dog Soldiers camp. We are here to help you with supplies and horses.

> BLACK KETTLE. As you can see, many of us are seriously injured. This is my wife on my shoulders. We will put the worst injured on the ponies, and the rest of us will walk. Thanks to you, our sick can have food and all can be kept warm with larger fires and buffalo robes tonight. Please, let me have one of your ponies for my wife, Medicine Woman Later, and we will continue our journey for the Dog Soldiers camp.

A horse is brought over, and Medicine Woman Later is laid on top. Several others are helped or lifted up onto the backs of other ponies, including George Bent. The rest walk or limp onward. When they reach the Dog Soldiers camp, many of the people there are related to Black Kettle's tribe. There is such wailing that has never been heard before.

> GEORGE BENT, *to Dog Soldiers.* I have seen a massacre of the innocents of my tribe. This will not go unavenged. I am going to join the Dog Soldiers, and together we will avenge the atrocities that occurred at Sand Creek.

> DOG SOLDIER. You and the others of your band are welcome to join us.

This day, many braves from Black Kettle's tribe join the Dog Soldiers, and they would proceed to destroy many homesteads and kill many White people, men, women, and children. They have learned well from the White man.

Back to Sheridan, Wyoming, 1918

JESSIE. You can see it here, Ed.

She lifts up one of her arthritic hands, pulls away the collar on her dress, and the scar becomes visible on the right side of her neck.

JESSIE. Like my grandma said, it is a reminder of
that day, that terrible day.

ED. It should have never happened. It was a crime
against humanity, and they know it. One of
their commanders, Captain Silas Soule, actually
testified at a congressional hearing about what
really happened at Sand Creek. Against orders,
he and his regiment never fired on the village
that day. He was then found murdered several
weeks later in Denver.

JESSIE. Perhaps there will be justice for what
happened to our tribe, but it will take many,
many years for the White man to realize that
they made a mistake, and more time will pass
before they will admit their mistake to us.

ED. It was after Sand Creek that your family
decided to move to a Fort. What was the name?

JESSIE. It was Fort D. A. Russell. A lot of Indian
families had decided that it was safer to remain
near the forts than to try to forage on our own.
Most of our menfolk had been killed in battle.

ED. You met Dad at Fort Laramie. Tell me more
about that as well.

Chapter 8

Keokuk, Lee County, Iowa, March 1, 1867

William has made the decision. He is meeting with Lieutenant Massey at Keokuk, Iowa, to enlist into the Fourth Infantry Regiment, Company A, Iowa. He is being interviewed in a private room. An enlistment card is being completed. Lieutenant Massey is older, in his thirties, of stocky build, and it looks like he saw some service in the Civil War as he has some scars on his face. He is in an Army uniform, the same style that was issued at that time.

LIEUTENANT MASSEY, *to William*. Full name.

WILLIAM. William Bixby.

LIEUTENANT. Age.

WILLIAM. Twenty-one.

LIEUTENANT. Place of birth.

WILLIAM. Lee County, Iowa.

THE lieutenant takes a look at William's physique.

LIEUTENANT. It looks like your hair is reddish brown, you're slender, your eyes are gray, and you have a ruddy complexion. What is your height?

WILLIAM. I don't know

LIEUTENANT. We can take care of that.

He places his pen down, gets up from his chair, and opens up a drawer. He takes out a measuring tape and runs it from head to foot

LIEUTENANT. Looks like five feet, ten inches.

WILLIAM. Gee, that is the same as my brother Aaron.

LIEUTENANT. Now, your service will be for three years. You'll be paid once a month, $13 per month. Do you have any skills?

WILLIAM. I've done a lot of farm work, but I can also drive a four-horse freight wagon.

LIEUTENANT. Well, that will come in handy. They always need good and fast freighters between the forts. Do you have any beneficiaries, next of kin in case of an emergency?

WILLIAM. My brother James Bixby, who lives at Jefferson Township, Lee County, Iowa.

LIEUTENANT. Do you have any questions?

WILLIAM. Yes. Do you know what the assignment
will be?

LIEUTENANT. Yes, I do. You are going to be
assigned to build a new fort in the Wyoming
Territory. They are going to name it Fort
Fetterman, after Captain William Fetterman,
who was massacred by the Indians with his
entire unit on December 21, 1866. The
Union Pacific Railway is making their Western
headquarters at Cheyenne, Wyoming Territory,
where Fort D. A. Russell is also being built. The
Bozeman Trail goes north, toward the Black
Hills, and we have to keep settlers from going
there. As long as we keep the treaty, the Indians
will allow settlers to travel down the Oregon
Trail in peace.

WILLIAM. Isn't the Bozeman Trail the one
that gold miners take to get to the Colorado
Territory?

LIEUTENANT. Yes, it is.

WILLIAM. Won't that be hard to keep people away
from?

LIEUTENANT. Yes, it will.

WILLIAM. I'm ready for service, sir.

LIEUTENANT. Good. We are leaving in a few
days with the other recruits.

The Forts in Wyoming Territory

After the Railroad Act of 1862, President Lincoln decides that military posts are needed to protect the railroad and the nation's interest from "hostile" forces. On July 4, 1867, the Union Pacific Railroad locates their Mountain Region headquarters at Crow Creek, later to be known as Cheyenne, Wyoming. A few months before this, the US Cavalry began the building of Fort D. A. (David Allen) Russell and Fort Fetterman to protect the railroad. They are both finished on July 4, 1867, to coincide with the opening of the Pacific Railroad's Mountain Region headquarters. Fort Laramie was already there, having been taken over by the US Army in 1849. Before that, it had been a fur Trading Post and had been known by the Indians for many decades. Fort Fetterman is at the juncture of the Bozeman Trail and the Oregon Trail. It is located on the south side of the Platte River.

Union Pacific Railway, Train Headed from Iowa City Iowa to Fort Laramie, Wyoming Territory, May 1867

There is a steam engine, with billowing smoke, rushing down the tracks. Attached are cars full of new recruits for the Cavalry and Infantry. There are also some cars with horses, wagons, and supplies. They are all headed through Crow Creek, Dakota Territory (eventually to be renamed Cheyenne, Wyoming Territory), into Fort Laramie. Inside one of the cars is a crowd of recruits, all talking to one another.

> WILLIAM, *to fellow recruit.* Wow, look at all that flatland! It seems so bleak in areas. You have to wonder how anyone can live here.

> RECRUIT. Yeah, it makes you wonder why the Indians are fighting so hard to keep it.

> WILLIAM. Look at that beast! That must be the buffalo I have heard so much about. There must

be millions of them. Look at how they run up
that hill and then back down. The little calves
are keeping up with their moms.

RECRUIT. I hear that we get coats and boots made
from them. They last a long time. They make
good robes and blankets. I saw some that were
sent out East. I'm William George Harris, by
the way. Everyone calls me George.

He extends his hand, and William responds by grasping his.

WILLIAM. I'm William Bixby. I come from Iowa.
Where are you coming from? You have an
accent.

GEORGE. Well, I originally came from England to
New York, but it was just too overcrowded. Too
many immigrants…

They both laugh.

GEORGE. I thought I would come out West to see
the open country. And boy, is it open!

WILLIAM. Were you recruited in New York?

GEORGE. No, I was actually in Iowa City, trying
to decide if I wanted to go by wagon train along
the Oregon Trail. It was there that I saw the
Cavalry recruiter, so I joined up. I did a lot of
horseback riding in England. This way, I get
paid to travel. It's the best of both worlds!

WILLIAM. I joined the infantry.

The train whistle starts to blow, and they can tell the train is starting to slow down. They are almost to their destination, Fort Laramie.

WILLIAM. We must be getting close.

GEORGE. I feel a little creeped out that the fort we
     will be building is named after a man who was
     massacred by the Indians.

WILLIAM. Yeah, and we have to protect the
     railroad workers and retrieve stolen animals
     from the Indians.

Just then, there is a screeching as the brakes start to take hold. The men sway in their seats as it finally comes to a halt. Suddenly, a man in uniform jumps up from the front seat and starts giving orders out in a very load voice.

LIEUTENANT. Listen to me closely. We are going
     to leave the train quickly. Those that have been
     selected for the Cavalry will go to the North,
     my left. (He points his left hand out the doorway.)
     And those that are Infantry, go to the South, my
     right. (He points his right hand out the doorway.)
     You'll get further instructions.

Everyone gets up and starts out. George heads north, and William heads south. As William gets out, he can see Fort Laramie. He can see some tepees in the distance.

LIEUTENANT. We need to unload the wagons
     first, then the supplies. Leave enough in each
     wagon for three men to sit at the edge of the
     wagon. Two people will sit up front.

All those that indicated on their registration form that they were freighters, please raise your hand.

William raises his hand, with about five others.

> LIEUTENANT. Those that raised their hand will
> be driving the wagons to our new location.
> There are not enough, so I will need to get
> some experienced freighters from the Cavalry.
> Go ahead and start getting the wagons out.
> You need to work as a team. Do not drop them
> down the side of the ramp.

He leaves them and walks around the engine to the other side. Eventually, he has five more men, including George, to help with the remaining wagons. The Cavalry recruits had taken the Cavalry horses and freighter horses off the other cars along with their bridles, blankets, and saddles. Now the Cavalry men who have been volunteered as freighters have the horses that will be hitched to the wagons and the horses that will become their mounts. They are all branded with US. They will be tied to the end of the wagons. The wagon horses will be fitted with the wagons after they are all taken out of the cars, which is easier said than done. The only blessing in getting the wagons out of the cars is that it is all downhill. One of the wagons loses control as it is being lowered and falls off the side of the ramp. It breaks a wheel. The lieutenant has a lot of words to describe his displeasure. The men involved could only dream of the horrible things they would be made to do once they get to the camp location.

> LIEUTENANT. I cannot believe that you four men
> could not get that wagon down in one piece.
> When we get to our camp, I want the four of
> you to come to me, and I will have a special
> assignment for you. Get in here, Andrew.

He points to a hefty man helping another set of men to get another wagon down. He finishes helping to get the wagon down the ramp, then runs over.

ANDREW. Yes, sir.

LIEUTENANT. We need you to repair this
    wheel. We have some repair equipment in
    the supply car. Go over to the sixth car down
    and you will find some square crates that have
    [BLACKSMITH] stenciled on them. They're
    heavy, so get some help. Get this wagon repaired
    as soon as possible.

ANDREW. Yes, sir, right away.

In the meantime, all the wagons have been unloaded from the train and supplies are being placed into them: flat boards, plaster, nails, food, kitchen supplies, stoves, lanterns, tents, and clothing are all loaded. The flat boards are bundled together. After a few hours of this, everyone is totally exhausted. Water is passed around for all to drink. They also are given some salt tablets due to the heat. The wagon wheel has been fixed, and the wagons are lined up to leave Fort Laramie. The officers and Cavalry are first, then the wagons. Many of the Cavalry horses are less than happy to have "strangers" on their backs, and some begin to snort and buck. The men would hoot and holler to encourage the recruit to stay on the horse, but many of them are thrown off and have to remount. Eventually, every private is able to stay on their mounts.

WILLIAM, *to George.* Look, over there! One of the
    horses is beginning to buck.

GEORGE. Oops, there he goes, plunk into the
    dust!

WILLIAM. That makes my butt hurt just looking
at it.

GEORGE. He's getting back up.

GEORGE, *to recruit.* Come on, man, you can do it!

GEORGE, *to William.* That horse is really jumping.
(*Pause.)* It looks like he won. The horse is
calming down. I wonder what my horse will do
once I get on him. They gave me a bigger one as
I'm kind of big.

WILLIAM. You can say that again!

GEORGE. Hey…

MAJOR WILLIAM MCEMERY DYE, *to the
lieutenant.* Along with the new recruits, we
have some men from Fort Laramie and Fort
Russell. These are men that have deserted or had
problems under command. They are being sent
to us because our fort is so far away it will be
hard to desert. If they try to escape, the Indians
will get them.

LIEUTENANT. Don't worry, sir, I'll keep a good
eye on them.

Once the officers and Cavalry start out, the wagons with the Infantry
men sitting on the back head out. Usually, the infantry would be forced
to walk, but the men have not been issued their uniforms or shoes, and
at this point the officers want everyone to arrive together, and they want
an uneventful trek to their new locations; the faster, the better.

William has started his wagon, and George is alongside. They look
at each other. It is at this time William sees the true advantage to having

a mustache like George's, as it would have protected his lips from the harsh sun and winds, and the dust later on the trek. He decides he will start growing one today.

> WILLIAM, *to George.* I like your mustache. It's nice and bushy.

> GEORGE. Yeah, I like it, especially right now in this heat and dust. It protects my nose from the dust and protects my lips from sunburn. In winter, it protects my nose from the wind and protects my lips from the cold.

> WILLIAM. I'm going to grow one right away.

> GEORGE. I believe it will make you feel and look better. Out here it is going to be essential to our health.

The men eventually come to the plateau that is to be their new home for the next three years (the period of their enlistment). The North Platte River runs down one side and then the next side as it meanders down the valley floor. The fort can be well defended, and they will have plenty of water. The only problem is that the water has to be transported from the bottom of the plateau to the top each day. Runs have to be made in the morning and in the afternoon. Once the water is loaded into large barrels in wagons at the bottom, the wagons have to be brought up the embankments to the fort. Then the water has to be distributed to the horse troughs and to the kitchen and to each barracks. This is the job that the men who dropped the wagon down the ramp have to do for the next week. Tents are set up by the men to protect the supplies and to sleep in until cabins could be made. The men involved with the construction of the cabins will get an extra thirty-five cents per day, and William and George both plan on getting the extra money.

The next day, uniforms are given out to the men. The Infantry have dark-blue jerseys, while the Cavalry have dark-blue blouses and sky-blue trousers. They are issued three gloves each, two right and one left, made of seal. Their boots go up to the knee and are made of stitched buffalo hide. Stockings would be just general issue, or you could get worsted socks for forty-one cents per pair. It is advised to get worsted socks to protect your feet from moisture, and during the winter months, it would keep your feet warmer. In the blazing heat of June, it is hard to believe just how hostile the winters are going to be.

William has gone up to the line forming for uniforms. He then approaches the first man.

FIRST MAN. Blanket.

WILLIAM grabs it and goes on.

SECOND MAN. How tall?

WILLIAM. Five feet, ten inches.

SECOND MAN. Here, take this.

He shoves a dark-blue shirt and dark-blue pants at him, which are laid on top of the blanket. William goes to the next man.

THIRD MAN. What size hat?

WILLIAM. That's 17 1/8.

A hat is handed to him. He tries it on, and it fits.

FOURTH MANs. What size shoe? William.
Ah, 13.

A big pair of shoes is laid on his uniform, and things are starting to get a little wobbly.

FIFTH MAN. Here are your gloves, two right and
    one left. You'll find that your right glove will
    have more use and wear out more often. Be
    good to them. They are made of seal.

William moves on for the last man.

SIXTH MAN. Do you want regular socks or
    worsted socks? Worsted cost forty-one cents a
    pair.

WILLIAM. I want worsted.

He tries to get into his pocket to get the money out, and his boots
land on the ground along with his gloves. He bends over to pick them
up. His hat falls off. There is a harsh comment made by the man beside
him, but William can't make it out.

He gets all his items and then gets his money out and places some
on the counter.

WILLIAM. Here you go, forty-five cents.

SIXTH MAN. Your change, four pennies.

He carries all the items and gets to his tent. He starts to change into
his clothes. As he does, he also pulls out his watch from his old pants
and places them into his new pants. His watch is there for him to look
at whenever he gets to thinking about his past and his family.

Chapter 9

Fort Fetterman, 1867

The building of the fort becomes a labor of love. They take pride in their ability to make something out of nothing. The officers actually have the enlisted men build their part of the fort first, then the officers' barracks, corrals and stables for the horses, and then kitchen facilities and laundry areas. Unlike most of the other forts, they would not have help from the Indians. Every nineteen men can have a laundress, and this person is usually the wife of one of the officers or the enlisted men. They also got a salary. Due to the shape of the plateau, the building is more rectangular. Fort D. A. Russell, being built at the same time, is diamond shaped. Enlisted men are also building this fort. The timing for the completion of both forts is set for the same day, July 4, 1867, and they are both completed on time.

Supplies for Fort Fetterman are much harder to get than they are for Fort Laramie and Fort D. A. Russell. The other two forts were near the Railway. To get supplies for Fort Fetterman meant freight men have to travel distant unimproved roads to Fort Laramie. Most of the supply orders include lanterns and stoves, which are of poor quality and have to be replaced often.

> QUARTERMASTER, *to George.* George, I need
> you to travel from Fort Fetterman to Fort
> Laramie to pick up supplies that we have

ordered. Here is a list. Be sure to mark off each item that you place in the wagon to be sure that we get everything we are entitled to. It will take you a full day to get there and a full day to get back. We have set up lodging for you at Fort Laramie.

GEORGE. Yes, sir. Am I to go alone, or do I have an escort?

QUARTERMASTER. You have very little of value in your wagon on the trip to Laramie, mostly mail from the fort. But you could have issues heading back as your wagon will be full of supplies. I'll assign William Bixby. He can also run the wagon if you are injured.

GEORGE. I don't plan on getting injured, sir.

He gives a smirk.

QUARTERMASTER. You better get going. Private Bixby has been told of his escort duties and is waiting for you at the stables.

George hurriedly runs to the stables and meets up with William.

GEORGE, to William. Imagine us being placed together. What luck! If we do well on this first trip, we could be asked to do this all the time. That certainly will cut down on the boredom of marching around in this hot, arid no-man's-land, and we get an extra four dollars per month!

WILLIAM. Well, I kind of overheard the officers
      talking about who would be the best team to
      send out, and I kind of volunteered us.

GEORGE. You are one smart man. Let's go!

They start out from the fort, the one they have built with their own
hands. They smile as they head through the gates and down the trail.

GEORGE. I've heard there is a place that we can
      go to have some fun while in Fort Laramie. It
      is called Hogs Ranch. I plan on heading over
      there. Want to come along?

WILLIAM. Well, I only hesitate a little because I
      don't really drink. I guess it is my brotherin-law's
      lifestyle. He was a Mormon.

GEORGE. I heard about the Mormons and their
      exodus. Did he go to Utah?

WILLIAM. No, there were followers in Iowa. He
      joined the Union Army and died at Vicksburg.

GEORGE. Oh, I'm sorry to hear that. I heard of
      this conflict right before I came over, the Union
      and Confederates, the Yankees and the Rebels.
      I heard it tore families apart. I'm surprised your
      government didn't just blow apart. But then
      over in England we were surprised that you won
      the Revolutionary War. If nothing else, your
      country is resilient.

WILLIAM. That we are. I think I'll let you have fun
      at Hogs Ranch, and I will simply go to the fort
      and rest for the journey back tomorrow.

GEORGE. Hey, why don't we go over to the
    Trading Post when we arrive?

WILLIAM. Okay.

He whips the reins just a little bit to get the horses going a little faster.
Upon their arrival at Fort Laramie, they both work hard to inventory
the items and to get the supplies into the wagon. It is a lot, and for a
moment they don't think it is going to all fit.

GEORGE. Phew, I didn't think it was going to all
    fit! You have some really good packing skills!

WILLIAM. I had a lot of experience putting
    supplies into the wagon in Montrose, Iowa.
    They had quite a business there, and a big need
    for freighters that could pack a good wagonload.

GEORGE. Well, we will make sure the wagon
    is secure, and then I am headed over to the
    Trading Post. Ya coming?

WILLIAM. You bet!

The wagon is secured inside the fort, and George heads out with
William for the Trading Post. It is just at the entrance of the fort. What
they see is pure chaos. There are enlisted men obtaining some items
they want, perhaps for their sweetheart in town. There were freighters,
teamster, and immigrants. There are Indians of all types, Cheyenne,
Sioux, and one Indian they had no idea which tribe he may have belonged
to. The squaws are holding out their blanket or skirts or blouses to have
flour, rice, tobacco, or sugar placed into it. There are children of all
sizes, some of whom are naked. The infants are in papoose cradles, and
the younger toddlers are picking up broken crackers off the floor to eat.
There are peppermint sticks that the older children like, but next to the
children, there is also a rather-large and tall enlisted man licking on one.

It makes the children chuckle. There are full leather outfits, like what a frontiersman would wear, and uniforms, and calicos with bright colors. Customers wear beaded outfits, their hair with feathers of hawks and eagles placed into them. A metal coin on one man shows he is a Peace Chief that has gone to Washington, DC. There are people trying to buy tobacco and pipes and matches, glass beads, household items. The Indians are very good bargainers and would communicate in English or sometimes sign language. The owner takes it all in stride. He has, in fact, been doing it for many decades.

> GEORGE, *to the owner.* Hi, I'm Private George Harris, Cavalry, at Fort Fetterman. You look really busy.

> OWNER. Yep, I've been working here for twenty years, back when it was called Sutler's Post. You see just about everything around here. I'm Seth Ward, the owner. Glad to meet you.

He reaches over and shakes George's hand.

> GEORGE. I and my partner, William Bixby, are going to be here for the night, and I want to rent a horse. How much?

> SETH WARD. Here is a sheet you need to complete. The fee is $5. When you bring the horse back, you get $3 back. That includes the reins and blanket and saddle. If you lose any of these items, you may owe more. Same thing if you bring back the horse in poor condition. You won't get the $3 back.

> GEORGE. That sounds good to me. And how much are the peppermint sticks?

SETH. Three for one penny.

GEORGE. Here is the form back. And I'll take
three. Here is the $5.01.

SETH. Thank you. Go around to the stables with
this invoice and they will get you all ready.
Anything else for you, sir?

He looks at William. George is handing him one of the peppermint
candy sticks.

WILLIAM. No, thank you.

They leave the Trading Post.

GEORGE, *to William.* Well, I am headed for some
fun and relaxation. I'll take this invoice over
to the stable and get the horse. See you later
tonight!

WILLIAM. Have fun.

GEORGE. Try not to let the bedbugs bite.

Little does George know that his night would conclude with an
Indian girl in his arms.
Jessie Continues Her Story

Fort D. A. Russell

JESSIE. We started living at Fort D. A. Russell. It
was brand-new, having been completed on July
4, 1867. We would help the soldiers with their
daily chores, like laundry and cooking, and they
would pay us a small amount so that we could

buy items that we needed. Sometimes we went
to Fort Laramie to buy items, which also meant
that we could visit relatives that lived there. It
was during this time that Sallie met Captain
James Cahill, who was in charge of the Second
Cavalry, Company K, at Fort D. A. Russell.

Sallie and Jessie are sitting on a buffalo hide on one side of the tepee,
while their mother and grandmother are on the other side on buffalo
hides. A small fire keeps the tepee warm, the smoke billowing upward
through the opening at the top. There are several tepees around the fort,
inhabited mostly by women that have lost their braves.

> JOSIE, *to the children.* We should stay together. We
> should never be alone. I have heard of many bad
> things that happen to young Indian maidens
> when they are alone in or near the forts.

> MINIHIE, *to the children.* Listen to us. I know you
> are growing up so fast and you feel that you can
> handle any situation, but following this rule can
> save your life.

> SALLIE. I am a woman now, and I need to make
> my own decisions. I have met a White soldier in
> uniform that has told me that he wants to marry
> me. You met him when he brought laundry
> down from the fort. His name is Captain James
> Cahill. I will meet him alone if he wants me to.

> JOSIE. I remember this man. He was drunk and
> smelled of whiskey. I have seen many of our
> young men take the same road. It only leads to
> violence, jail, or death. Please, Sallie, consider
> your choices.

SALLIE. He is a Captain of the Cavalry, and I will
make him a wonderful wife. Please, I want your
blessing.

MINIHIE. The only reason we hesitate is that we
fear for your safety. We love you and want you
to be safe. You must make this decision on
your own.

SALLIE. Then I am leaving now to meet him. I love
you all!

Sallie gets up and leaves the tepee. The women have anguish and worry. Jessie is still young but understands her sister's desire to be with a White man who can provide for her and their children.

Hogs Ranch That Night

Sally and James have gone to the Hogs Ranch, where servicemen go to drink when they are on leave. James has been drinking a lot and is drunk. The building is full of noise and glasses clinging and smoke.

JAMES, *to Sallie*. Come on, let's go outside and get
some air.

They then reach a wooded area, and he pulls Sallie close. She assumes he would kiss her and hold her like he has done before. But this time the alcohol has taken over and he wants the power and control over her and the situation. He wants to have sex, but she resists, now realizing that she is in a place she would not be able to escape.

JAMES. I want you now. You've been teasing me for
days!

SALLIE. But, James, you told me that we would be
married, that we would be husband and wife!

JAMES. You bitch! You squaw, what makes you
    believe I would ever marry a savage? If you won't
    give it to me, I'll take it from you!

SALLIE. No, don't. I can't believe you can do this
    to me!

He starts hurting her and hitting her, and then he starts ripping her clothes off.

He unleashes his belt and pants and throws her into the ground. Her head hits a tree. Before she can get back up, he is on top of her and is raping her. It is then she sees the large body of George come in and pull James off her. He hits James in the face several times. Others run in and takes James away, fearing that George might kill him.

JAMES. She is just a squaw, an animal. I can do
    anything I want with her. Why, we're killing
    them all over the plains. Why not her?

He wipes his face with his hands to get some of the blood out of his eyes, nose, and mouth. She remembers George swearing at James.

GEORGE. You bastard! You can't get away with
    this! Even if she is Indian, she is a human being.
    You're the animal, and I'll make sure that you
    stand trial for this!

It is George who bends down, asks her if she is okay, and scoops her up to take her back to her family. He carefully gets her on his horse. It is a long way, but he walks the horse slowly so as not to hurt her.

A full day has elapsed and the sun is coming up when there is a commotion outside Josie's tepee. Minihie gets up from her buffalo robe blanket to see what is happening. A husky, muscular young White soldier with a large mustache, in a Cavalry uniform, has Sallie on his horse. He reaches up, carefully pulls her down and into his arms. She has been beaten, and her clothes are ripped. But she is alive. Minihie calls out to her mother, Josie.

> MINIHIE. Mom, come quickly. Something has
> happened to Sallie!

Josie quickly gets up and runs out to see Minihie crying over her daughter in the man's arms.

> MINIHIE. What has happened? Who are you?
> How did you come to be holding her in your
> arms? What have you done?

She looks up into the eyes of the White man, with hatred in her face.

> GEORGE HARRIS. My name is Private George
> Harris, Cavalry. I was witness to a horrible sight.
> Your daughter was being attacked by Captain
> James Cahill. I pulled him off her and subdued
> him. I was told by others that came to help that
> she belonged to this tepee. I want you to know
> that Captain Cahill has been arrested and he
> will have a trial for what he has done. In the
> meantime, I have brought her back to you. We
> will send a doctor down from the fort to help in
> her care.

> JOSIE. No, we do not want any more of the White
> man's help. We can care for her on our own.
> Leave my granddaughter, *now!*

He hands the girl over to her mother. As he turns around, you can see that his knuckles on both hands are bruised and bloodied from having hit someone several times. He starts to get up on his horse but then turns around to see the family carrying the girl into the tepee. He has a deep desire to help them. He gets up on his horse for the ride back to

Fort Laramie. He needs to return this horse and get back to his wagon of supplies for the long journey back to Fort Fetterman.

Minihie sobs, knowing that something horrible and life-changing has occurred. Minihie and Josie carry Sallie into the tepee and lay her on one of the buffalo robes. As they examine and clean her wounds, they discover that she has been violated. Their hearts are broken.

> MINIHIE. My poor, sweet daughter. I knew
> something like this would happen. White men
> feel that they can do anything to us.

> JOSIE. We did our best to warn her. She made a
> decision that will change all our lives.

Jessie has not said a word and sits in almost a trance state. She rocks back and forth. Her sister is wounded and might even die from her injuries. The White man has struck again.

Fort Laramie to Fort Fetterman That Morning

George heads back to Fort Laramie after helping Sallie return to her mother's tepee. He has not had any sleep but knows that they must take the wagon back to Fort Fetterman. He gets into Fort Laramie and returns the horse he has rented. He starts to walk over to where the wagon has been stored. The horses are already hitched up and ready to go. He walks up to William.

> WILLIAM. Hey, George. It looks like you have
> been out all night. You look terrible! Hey, what
> happened to your knuckles? You been in a fight?

> GEORGE. Yeah, you won't believe it. I rescued a
> young Northern Cheyenne Indian girl from
> certain death at the hands of a Captain from
> Fort D. A. Russell. He had way too much to

drink and was beating up this poor girl. I had
to drag him off her, and I was so mad. Well, I
almost killed him. Didn't help my knuckles any,
and I didn't get any sleep. I had to get her back
to her family's tepee on the outskirts of Fort
Russell. That was a long way away. Poor thing.
And her family was really upset. I think they
believe I had something to do with it. Maybe
next time we come into Fort Laramie I can
check on her at Fort Russell.

WILLIAM. Sounds like you're really involved with
this girl. Maybe I can meet her and her family.
I would like to make some contact with the
Northern Cheyenne and maybe even learn their
language. I hear interpreters make a lot more
money than enlisted men.

GEORGE. Well, let me get a quick snack, clean off
my knuckles, and we can get out of here. If we
are much later, I'm afraid they won't let us take
in the wagons again. And by the way, can you
do most of the driving back? I'm a little bushed?

WILLIAM. Okay, but you owe me one.

George is sound asleep, snoring loudly, as they head back. William
begins to feel like they are being watched. Sure enough, he begins to
see some Indians on their ponies up on a ridge. He pokes George with
his elbow.

WILLIAM. Hey, George, wake up. I see some
Indians on that rise.

He points over to the area where there is still dust from where they had been.

> GEORGE. I see where they are by their dust.
> I'm getting the rifle out. Are you good with
> firearms?

> WILLIAM. Yeah, I had to shoot wild game for my
> meals when I was young. I'm pretty good.

> GEORGE. Then I'm going to take the reins, and
> you take the rifle.

William and George exchange. He whips the horses a little to have them start running. Then they see the Indians coming closer around a bend.

> WILLIAM. Jeez, they are getting closer.

Soon the Indians are near enough that an arrow has hit the wagon. George looks back at the wagon with a surprised look to see the arrow sticking to the side.

> GEORGE. Well, at least we have a good story for
> being a little late.

William aims the rifle and takes his first shots. George whips the horses more, and they are running, lathering under their harness and foaming at their bits. Luckily, the Indians pull up on their horses' reins and start to fall back. They then gallop back up the hillside to the ridge.

> WILLIAM. Boy, that was close! I don't think it was
> my shooting that scared them off. I think we
> were just too close to the fort for comfort.

George slows down so the horses don't wear out, and they soon reach the fort. There is quite a commotion when the wagon hits the guard gate with an arrow stuck to the side. Soon, George and William are the talk of the fort. They are the first men to have a run-in with the Cheyenne savages. They take the wagon to the quartermaster, and all the supplies are in order as they are checked off the list and placed out of the wagon. He is pleased with their work and with the fact that after being attacked by Indians, the supplies are safe.

> QUARTERMASTER. You two did a great job of
> guarding the supplies back to the fort, and they
> are all in order. It is exactly what I ordered. We
> probably will need another load in two weeks.
> You two up to trying this again?

WILLIAM and GEORGE. Yes, sir!

Fort Fetterman, Wyoming Territory, 1867

Once George returns to Fort Fetterman, he has to explain to his commanding officer what happened at the Hogs Ranch and that he was the main material witness for charges against Captain James Cahill.

> GEORGE, *to Brigadier General H. W. Wessells.* Sir,
> thank you for taking the time to listen to me.
> I realize that you have just taken over for our
> previous commander, Major William McEmery
> Dye. I find myself in a difficult situation. I
> had to rescue a young Indian maiden from
> being raped by one of the officers assigned to
> Fort D. A. Russell. I filed charges against him
> for disorderly conduct, as he was very drunk
> in a public place while in uniform. I also filed
> charges for the rape of a civilian. I realize that
> we are soldiers and that at times we are actually

killing hostile Indians, but this behavior is unbecoming of an officer who has vowed to uphold the laws of this territory and the laws of the military.

BRIGADIER GENERAL. You realize that testifying against an officer will be very hard on your career in the service and that others may backlash and even harm you, right? I do not know if I can protect you if you insist on going through with a trial.

GEORGE. Currently, he is under arrest. He had just been transferred from Fort Laramie to Fort D. A. Russell a week before. I think he was celebrating his promotion to Captain of the Cavalry.

BRIGADIER GENERAL. I know Captain Cahill. He fought bravely in the Civil War. He has been with the Army for many years. He has moved through several forts, always wanting to be closer to the action. But I believe his drinking has finally compromised his ability to serve.

GEORGE. I will need to go back within the week to file formal charges and start the process for a trial. Do I have your permission, sir?

BRIGADIER GENERAL. Are you sure you want to go through with this?

GEORGE. Yes, I need to pursue this injustice.

BRIGADIER GENERAL. Very well, you can take a leave on Thursday of next week.

Fort D. A. Russell, Three Days Later

As the following week comes, George mounts his horse and goes to Fort Russell. It is a lot faster and easier without a wagon. He turns his horse over to the stables.

> GEROGE, *to Stable Hand.* Which way to the
> Captain's quarters?

> STABLE HAND. It's way over in that two-story
> barracks with the porch.

> GEORGE. Thanks!

George walks through the parade ground. There is a tall pole with an American flag waving in the wind. The buildings are laid out in a diamond shape. Cisterns full of water are located near the four corners.

> GEORGE, *softly to himself.* Lucky sons-of-a-gun.
> They don't need to fill barrels full of water all
> day long and then drag them up a steep bank
> to the top of a plateau. Wish we had a water
> system like this one.

He clomps up on the stairs of the officers' porch. He walks inside.

> GEORGE, *to the Private.* Where can I find the
> commander for the fort?

> PRIVATE. His office is the first door on the right.
> Who are you and what do you want?

> GEORGE. I'm Private George Harris, Cavalry, Fort
> Fetterman. I'm here to see him about Captain
> James Cahill.

The private does not look too happy with the visitor. He can guess what it concerns. The whole fort knows what it is about.

PRIVATE. Sit right here and I'll let Captain
Pettigrew know that you are here.

He points over to the bench, walks over to the Captain's door, and knocks.

CAPTAIN. Come in.

The private opens the door, walks in, and closes the door.

The Captain's office has a very nice decor. There are two very nice stuffed leather chairs, two bookcases full of books, a large oak desk, and another leather chair with a high back. This is where the commander sits. On his desk is a small lamp with a green glass top, an inkwell, and a pen. Papers are ordered in neat piles. His walls have a lithograph of the President and a broadsword and a Union Civil War hat.

CAPTAIN. What is it, Private Kelly?

KELLY. There is a Private George Harris, Cavalry,
from Fort Fetterman, outside. He wishes to talk
to you about Captain Cahill.

CAPTAIN. I can tell this is going to be a long day.
Let him in.

Private Kelly leaves the room and returns with George.

CAPTAIN. You can leave, Private Kelly.

PRIVATE KELLY. Yes, sir.

He seems a little angry that he is not allowed to stay and slams the door behind him.

CAPTAIN. So, you are George Harris. You have made some serious charges against our Captain Cahill. You realize he is a decorated officer from the Civil War? He is a hero!

George tries to hold back his anger because "their" Captain Cahill is an animal.

GEORGE. Sir, it hurts me to be here today. But injustice needs to be exposed. A person that has perpetrated the injustice needs to be held accountable. You know the details of my testimony and those of the witnesses to that night. While wearing the uniform of the US Army, he was drunk. The first charge is that of disorderly conduct. He then raped a young Indian girl, a civilian.

CAPTAIN. Well, I also heard that Captain Cahill and this girl had seen each other a few times and that there was a marriage proposal. It would be hard to prove that they were not simply engaged in what men and women have done since the beginning of time. Plus, I've heard that Indian women simply throw themselves onto men in uniform.

George's face is turning red, and he is clenching his fists, which still bare injury from hitting the face of Captain Cahill.

GEORGE. Sir, I can assure you from the screams emanating from this young girl that there was

no willingness on her part that night. If she had
been a White girl instead of an Indian girl, there
wouldn't be any question about his guilt.

CAPTAIN. Well, all this effort may go to waste,
    I'm afraid. You see, after his arrest, Captain
    Cahill had a great need for alcohol and he
    had withdrawals. He had a seizure and hit his
    head. Because of the head injury and need for
    alcohol, he is very ill. We are not even sure if he
    will recover well enough to stand trial for any
    accusations you may have against him.

George looks a little shocked, almost speechless, and then a little
disappointed. He wants to take this man to trial and tell the world about
his drunkenness and shameful behavior.

GEORGE. If he recovers, will a messenger relay
    that information to Fort Fetterman?

CAPTAIN. Yes, I will do that if he recovers. At that
    time, we will take another look at the charges
    you have filed.

GEORGE. Thank you, sir.

He slowly leaves the decorated office and goes past the Private. The
Private turns.

PRIVATE KELLY, *whispering quietly.* That Indian
    squaw and her heathen family pulled up stakes
    and fled to Fort Laramie. I guess she couldn't
    take it from a real man.

He grins and chuckles. George turns around, faces the Private, shows his
fists newly scarred from the face of Captain Cahill. The Private jerks back.

> GEORGE, whispering. You're an animal, just like
>   your Captain Cahill!

He walks down the stairs and back to the stable. He retrieves his horse, places the blanket and saddle back on. As George cinches the saddle, he uses a little more force than necessary, releasing a little of his anger. He decides to ride to Fort Laramie.

Fort Laramie, Wyoming Territory, Same Day

George wants to see Sallie, to make sure she is okay. He figures if he has something to offer her family, he might be welcomed. He goes to the Trading Post. He isn't too interested in looking around and quickly sees a cast-iron skillet.

> GEORGE, *to owner, Seth Ward*. I'll take one of
>   those large cast-iron skillets.

> SETH. Well, we have been selling a lot of these now
>   that the two forts have been built. People are
>   starting to find me. Where are you from? Looks
>   like Fort D. A. Russell. Wait, I remember you
>   now. You're from Fort Fetterman.

> GEORGE. Right. How much?

> SETH. That's $5.

> GEORGE. Wow, that's a lot. Tell you what? I have
> $4 right here. See?

He pulls out exactly $4 in $1 bills.

> SETH. Hmm, okay, $4.

He gets the skillet down from the hook, wraps it in paper with a string. George takes it.

> GEORGE. Do you know where the tepee of
> Humpback Woman is?

> OWNER. They're new. I saw them move in about
> half a mile south on the other side of the river.
> The bridge across the river is that way.

His arms move over to the west. George heads for the bridge and has to ask an Indian woman where the tepee is. Eventually, he finds it.

Josie's Tepee, Fort Laramie, Same Day

Josie and Minihie decide to leave Fort D. A. Russell and move to Fort Laramie, Wyoming, where they could be away from the person who has brought such injury and disgrace upon Sallie.

> JOSIE, *to family*. Things are much better here at
> Fort Laramie, and we have more relatives here
> to help us, Minihie. We must always beware,
> however, of the White man. He can never be
> trusted.

She looks over at Sallie and Jessie to be sure they have heard her. They have. Sallie has lowered her head.

Just then, they hear some footsteps nearby and expect some men from the fort with laundry or food for them to cook. But it is not who they suspect. Instead, it is George Harris.

> MINIHIE. Hello, Private Harris.

> GEORGE. I am glad that you remember me. I
> wanted to check in on Sallie. Is she okay? I

heard that you moved to Fort Laramie, and I
wanted to know that she was all right.

MINIHIE. Yes, she thrives. We thank you for
helping her. Later, when we heard more details
about that night, we realized that I accused you
in error. If it had not been for you, our Sallie
might be dead.

GEORGE. I have something for your family. Is it
all right if I present it to all the members of your
household?

MINIHIE. Yes. Let me get them.

She goes back into the tepee, and they all come out. Sallie stays
behind her mother and grandmother, but Jessie is right up front, showing
a lot of curiosity. George pulls out a brown paper package with a string
around it. He presents it to Josie, out of respect, as she is the eldest.

Josie cradles the heavy object in her hands and unwraps the item.
She gasps as she realizes that it is a cast-iron skillet. She looks up into
George's eyes and sees that this is actual kindness. He is giving them
something that will help them eat healthy and be able to earn some
money so they can cook for others.

JOSIE. I think you know what this means. It is
appreciated, and we thank you very much.

MINIHIE. Yes, we are grateful.

MINIHIE gives the children a stern look.

MINIHIE. Tell this kind gentleman thank you.

JESSIE AND SALLIE, *in unison*. Thank you,
Private Harris.

Sallie has pulled her head up and started to look George directly into the eyes. She now remembers some of what happened to her that night as a flashback. She remembers the fear of that night as well as the kindness and tenderness of his arms and hands as he protected her.

As Sallie looks at George and George looks at Sallie, there seems to be a bond, a spark of the love that they both have always hoped for.

> GEORGE, *to Sallie and her family.* It is nice to
> see you doing so well. I run freighters between
> Fort Fetterman and Fort Laramie. I will be here
> several times a month. Is it okay for me to visit
> with your family?

Josie can see the spark between Sallie and George as she looks at both of their faces.

> JOSIE, *to George.* Yes, you are welcome to visit.

Later, as they go into the tepee…

> JOSIE, *to Minihie.* I think we were wrong. Perhaps
> there is a White man we can trust.

Four Months Later

William and George are often selected to pick up supplies between Fort Fetterman and Fort Laramie. It seems like every two weeks they are headed on the road again. But George never has a chance to see Sallie again until about four months later. With their supply list and mail, they head down the trail. Soon they reach Fort Laramie.

> GEORGE. Well, that was fast. The more we do
> this, the faster we go.

> WILLIAM. Yeah, we seem to see the chuckholes
> before we get to them and can go faster without

breaking our butts. It also was a good idea
for you to have me check the wagon wheels,
attachments, and to select the best horses before
we left.

GEORGE. Yep. We have it down pat. Here we are.

He puts on the brakes after they pull into the fort. They get out at the supply storage area and start packing the wagon with the supplies from their list. It is getting much colder now, so there are more stoves. Packed into crates, they weigh a great deal.

WILLIAM. It sure is getting cold now. I'm glad
they are ordering enough stoves and kerosene.
Looks like we even have sperm oil this time.

GEORGE. This is heavy. It must be a stove. Give
me a little help.

As they both grasp the crate and lift, William's hand slips from underneath. The crate comes down with a big bang, just missing George's big toe.

GEORGE. Gee whiz, William, what ya trying to
do, make me a cripple?

WILLIAM. What's the problem? You have nine
more!

They both chuckle. They finally get everything packed in the wagon, and all is secured. The horses are placed into the stables for the night.

WILLIAM. You headed for the Hogs Ranch
tonight?

GEORGE. Nope! I learned my lesson. I'm headed
over to see Sallie's family, with her mom,
Minihie, and her grandmother Humpback
Woman.

WILLIAM. I remember you talking about them.
Can I come along? I want to learn Cheyenne,
and maybe they can teach me.

GEORGE. Sure. Let's stop at the Trading Post and
get some items they can use. Maybe if you have
a gift for the grandmother, she will trade for
some lessons.

They head over to the Trading Post. The same chaos is there, but
there are more blankets around the Indian's shoulders to keep them
warm. The enlisted men have their heavier coats and their hats on.

GEORGE. Hi, Seth. How's business?

SETH. Just great! With the two new forts, we are
getting a lot more business.

GEORGE. Well, I need a small paring knife and a
box of matches.

WILLIAM. And I need a larger knife. The kind you
can cut meat with, like a Bowie knife.

SETH. Here is the small knife and matches. That's
$3. I'm throwing in the box of matches as you
are a repeat customer. The larger knife is $5.

WILLIAM. Is it okay if I also get a pack of matches
for free? I promise I'll come back.

He smiles at Seth with a wink.

SETH. Okay, you drive a hard bargain.

He hands a box of matches to William. George lays out the $3 on the counter, and William places $5 down. Seth takes the items and wraps them in paper with a string across them.

George slaps William on the back in acknowledgment of his bargaining skills, and they walk toward Josie's tepee. They can see from the outside that the buffalo hide is painted with animals, such as buffalo, horses, and dogs. There are people, both Indian and uniformed White men. And there are stars, a moon, and a sun. The colors are black and red and yellow.

Minihie can hear their boot steps and walks to the outside flap.

> MINIHIE. Hello, George! It is good to see you.
> Can you smell the food that we are preparing?
> We are cooking it on the skillet you gave us.

> GEORGE. That smells great! What kind of meat is
> that? Deer?

> MINIHIE. No, it is elk. One of my relatives was
> able to shoot one. It is so hard to find live game
> nowadays. It is a true blessing.

She then looks at William with distrust.

> MINIHIE. Who is this man you have brought with
> you? I have never seen him before.

> GEORGE. This is my good friend Private William
> Bixby. Like me, he comes from Fort Fetterman.
> We have brought a wagon to fill with supplies,
> and we will be leaving tomorrow morning
> together.

WILLIAM. It is a pleasure to meet you.

He puts out his hand, but Minihie does not take it. She makes a small grunt and looks disgusted at his offer, so he slowly takes his hand back. At this point Josie has poked her face out of the tepee and sees George.

> JOSIE. So nice to see you! You are always welcome
> here. And who is this with you?

> GEORGE. My friend Private William Bixby.

> JOSIE. Well, any friend of George's is a friend
> of ours. Come in. Share our meal. We have
> wonderful elk for dinner.

> GEORGE. Thank you. We both have presents
> for you.

Josie's and Minihie's eyes brighten up and both head back into the tepee with George and William behind them. As George and William head in, they see Jessie and Sallie in one side of the tepee and Josie and Minihie have settled on another side. George sits next to Sallie and William, and William sits next to Josie and George. The skillet is in the center of the tepee on top of the fire. The smoke spirals upward out of the top. Items are organized neatly: water bucket, robes, places to sleep, cooking utensils, knives, and sacred items such as pouches. One can see from the outside the shadows of the people within the tent. The fire glows and flickers. Unlike most of the tepees now seen around the fort, this one is made from actual buffalo hide instead of canvas, supported by long pine lodgepoles.

> GEORGE. I have a gift for the family of
> Humpback Woman.

He hands the small wrapped package to her. She unwraps the package and sees the paring knife and matches. She looks up at George and smiles. He can see now that many of her teeth are missing.

> JOSIE. You continue your kindness to our family.
> The matches will allow us to start our fire
> quickly. These old hands of mine find it harder
> each year to use the traditional flint to start a
> fire.

She holds up her hands, showing the arthritis that is forming in them.

> WILLIAM. Humpback Woman, I would like
> to barter for something. I wish to learn the
> Cheyenne language, and I have an item for
> payment if you agree.

Josie looks at Minihie, Sallie, and Jessie. They nod to continue.

> JOSIE. Does it matter which one of us helps you
> learn the language? I and Minihie are very busy
> earning money, by helping the uniformed men
> with meals or their laundry, that we do not have
> the time.

> WILLIAM. I only ask that the person who teaches
> me know both English and Cheyenne. They also
> need to have great patience with me, for I am a
> slow learner.

> JOSIE. Let me see the item.

William hands her the larger package, and she cuts the string. She unwraps it. Her eyes and those of all in the tepee get big.

JOSE. Oh my, this is wonderful! It will allow
    us to cut large pieces of meat with ease. We
    can loan it to our family members so we can
    receive a share from the hunt. It is also great for
    protection!

Without hesitation, she grabs the handle and stabs the knife, as if
to kill an imaginary foe.

GEORGE, in surprise. I'm glad I'm not one of your
    enemies. I have a feeling you have used one of
    these before.

JOSIE. Oh yes, many times.

She looks into the eyes of William and George to emphasize that
she can care for her own safety.

JOSIE. Yes, your trade is good. Jessie will help you
    learn our language, and along the way, you will
    probably learn our customs as well.

Jessie smiles with delight at the new task she has been assigned. The
meat is done. There are some buffalo hide bowls.

JOSIE. It looks like the meat is done. Let me cut
    it and I will place it into our bowls. Here you
    go. Now, let's thank our higher spirit for this
    wonderful food!

They all take a moment for silence. The meat is picked up by their
fingers, and pieces are bitten off. As George is eating, his large arm and
elbow accidentally hit Sallie's food bowl and she has to get up to wipe
herself off and to retrieve her meal.

GEORGE. Oops! Sallie, I'm sorry. Here, let me
help.

It is then that George notices that Sallie is pregnant. He almost chokes
on his food in surprise. William looks up in confusion, trying to figure
out what is happening. Sallie has a sad look and turns around, crying.

GEORGE. Sallie, turn around, please. I understand
what has happened. None of this was your fault.
Please look at me.

Sallie wipes her tears and turns around. She then sits down.

SALLIE. I am so ashamed…

The tears start again.

GEORGE. Sallie, there is no shame for you. There
is shame on the White man that did this.
Captain Cahill needs to go to trial for this. The
last time I was here, I was filing charges against
him. But he has become ill.

Sallie immediately interrupts him. She now has distress for his
welfare on her face.

SALLIE. What is wrong?

GEORGE. Sallie, he is ill from drinking too
much. Since his arrest, he has had no alcohol.
His system needed the alcohol, so he had
withdrawal. It was so severe that he had a
seizure. He hit his head and is not recovering
well. He may never come out of it. There
probably will be no trial for what he did to you,

but he will get what he deserves in the end.
Sallie, this is the third time I have met with you.

George looks over to Josie and Minihie and then looks directly into Sallie's eyes.

> GEORGE. I care for you very much. I want to get
> to know you. We can wait until after the baby is
> born to make any decisions for our future, but I
> want to be your helper and your protector.

He reaches out his hand, but Sallie is still too ashamed to accept it.

> MINIHIE. You speak wisely. We will see what
> happens to Captain Cahill and with Sallie after
> the birth of the child.

> JOSIE. Yes, George, we appreciate the way you are
> handling this, and I agree that we should wait
> to see what happens in the next few months.
> Right now, it is time to go. We need our rest for
> tomorrow's work.

> GEORGE. By all means, we need to go. Thank you
> so much for the meal. We head back to Fort
> Fetterman tomorrow morning. If all goes well,
> we will be back in two weeks.

> WILLIAM. And perhaps I will have my first lesson
> in the Cheyenne language!

William looks at Jessie, who will be his tutor, and smiles at her. She smiles but turns her head in embarrassment. She seems so young, and yet he knows that she will be a good teacher.

As George and William leave the tepee and walk back to the fort, they have a conversation.

WILLIAM. Boy, that certainly complicates things
with Sallie having another man's child! How do
you really feel about this?

GEORGE. I think, the moment I held Sallie in my
arms that night, I fell in love with her. Her child
will be a part of the woman I love.

WILLIAM. Wow, George, that is so beautiful and
caring! Who would have ever thought you had it
in you…

William escapes before George can grab him. Eventually, they get
to the fort and find a barracks to sleep in.

Chapter 10

Life in Fort Fetterman, Winter 1867–1868

Life in the infantry is hard. William has to conduct drills that mean hikes into the empty prairie for one hundred miles out and one hundred miles back. Sometimes the Cavalry drills with them and George would be there. This is in all kinds of weather, blistering hot, torrential rain, snow and blizzards. It really gets cold in the winter, and William is glad he has his worsted socks and tall boots for the winter. They are also issued coats made with buffalo fur and hides. They keep you warm but are stinky after the rain.

Later, as they were camped…

> WILLIAM, *to George.* Man, this is the coldest
> weather I have ever been in! I can't believe they
> have us walking one hundred miles in the snow!
> At least you have a horse.

> GEORGE. I don't know if that is such an
> advantage. We are sitting high up, and the
> wind is just ferocious sometimes. The snow
> comes straight into my face. I'm glad I have
> a big mustache to cover up my nose and lip.
> Sometimes I even feel like I have icicles hanging
> down my chin!

WILLIAM. I'm glad I decided to buy the worsted socks. They are much warmer than regular Army socks. And when they get wet, my feet can still stay warm. I feel sorry for any of my unit that didn't get any.

GEORGE. The buffalo skin coats are great, but boy, do I stink when they get wet! A wet dog smells a lot better. But who am I to complain? At least I am warmer than most people with just wool coats.

WILLIAM. I agree.

Even during the winter, George and William are teamed up to drive the freighters for supplies. It dawns on George why.

GEORGE, *to William*. You know what, William?

WILLIAM. No, what?

GEORGE. I figured out why they want to send you and me to Fort Laramie to get supplies all the time.

WILLIAM. Why? Because they need more supplies?

GEORGE. No, you fool! The reason they pick us and usually no one else.

WILLIAM. I think it is because we do a good job and bring back the right items.

He can see when he looks at George that this is not the right answer.

WILLIAM. Okay, why?

GEORGE. Because we don't desert. You know
    Fort Fetterman is a hard place to serve in. We
    have lost a lot of men to desertion. Every time
    someone was sent out to bring something back
    from town or the railway, they disappeared.
    The commander is kind of getting used to it.
    But when they send us two, we never bolt. We
    always come back.

WILLIAM. Hmmm. Well, we will put in our three
    years of service and then we will be done. What
    will you do after your time is up?

GEORGE. I'm going to marry Sallie, take my free
    land, and work it. I'm going to become a big
    cattle baron. How about you, William?

WILLIAM. Well, there isn't much back in Iowa for
    me. If I were to take my free land for my service,
    I would want it out here.

Sometimes George and William have to escort riders or wagons for safety to other forts during the Indian uprising. The treaty has been broken, and Chief Red Cloud of the Lakota is on the warpath. Once they have reached the foreign fort, William and George could visit.

GEORGE. It's hard to believe that all this uprising
    started because of a Mormon cow. It strayed
    into an Indian village, and they ate it.

WILLIAM. Sounds like a reasonable thing to do
    when you are starving.

GEORGE. Then the owner got all uptight and
    wanted the Indian who killed and ate his cow
    to go to jail. The Indians even offered to pay for

the cow. But they would not give up the person who killed and ate the cow, because they all ate of the cow.

WILLIAM. It ended in tragedy for the Indians, as usual. White men shot many of them. Red Cloud was angered, and as the Lakota Chief, he wouldn't be happy until all the White men were out of his sight.

GEORGE. Did you hear? They made a new treaty.

WILLIAM. I heard a rumor, but I am glad to hear things will be better.

GEORGE. The government is actually going to close the Bozeman Trail and abandon all the forts north of the Platte River. Let's see, that would be Fort Smith, Fort Phil Kearney, and Fort Reno. Well, it is going to make our job a lot harder. We'll have to keep people from going up the Bozeman Trail, and it is the fastest way to get to the Colorado gold fields. How are we going to keep all those gold-hungry, feverish people from going that way?

WILLIAM. I guess we were lucky to have been built south of the North Platte River. Otherwise, we would be closing too.

GEORGE. Now that would just piss me off royally, after all the work we did to build those buildings ourselves.

WILLIAM. We can be real proud of our work. But I kind of understand now why the officers

had us build our barracks first. We could make
all the mistakes on our buildings as none of us
really knew how to build barracks. By the time
we got to theirs, we were experts.

GEORGE. Our barracks certainly are cold. Air gets
in from all directions.

WILLIAM. Yeah, I noticed that nice, cool breeze
coming through the walls the last time we slept
there. I guess that is what tar paper is for. Just
don't dump a lantern on it, or it will go up in
flames.

GEORGE. Well, at least it would be warmer at
night. Good night!

Fort Fetterman, February 6, 1868

That winter of 1867–1868 is harsh, and only a few trips to Laramie
could be made. Fort Fetterman is surprised when a messenger from Fort
Russell comes to call.

PRIVATE. I have a special delivery letter for Private
George Harris, Cavalry, from Captain Pettigrew
of Fort Russell.

He is guided to George's barracks.

PRIVATE. Sir, I have a special letter for you from
Captain Pettigrew of Fort Russell.

George accepts the letter, hoping it would tell him that Captain
Cahill is better and he could stand trial.

To: Pvt. George Harris, Cavalry, Ft. Fetterman From: Capt. Pettigrew, Ft. D. A. Russell

I wish to inform you of the death of Capt. James Cahill on February 5, 1868, at Fort D. A. Russell. He died of dementia tremors.

GEORGE. Thank you, Private. You can go
back now.

Of course, having a special delivery letter causes quite a ruckus. Everyone wants to know what it is all about.

GEORGE. None of your business!

George is anxious to be assigned to the next supply wagon, so he could see Sallie. He isn't sure if she would find out, and he wants to be there for her. One week later, he gets the chance and is paired with William. On the way to Fort Laramie, George and William have a conversation.

WILLIAM. I bet that was quite a shock to hear that
Captain Cahill had died. I was not expecting
that. Were you?

GEORGE. No. But maybe it is for the best. Sallie
is kind of like a widow now. There isn't anyone
else in her life but me.

WILLIAM. Boy, you've got this lovesickness bad!
The family still wants you to wait for after the
birth of the baby. Really, George, maybe you
ought to wait until after your service is over.

GEORGE. I just want what's best for her and the
baby. I wonder if it will be a girl or a boy.

Later, after the supplies are all accounted for, George and William walk to Humpback Woman's tepee. When they get close, the familiar figure of Minihie could be seen at the flap.

> MINIHIE. You two would never be good at
> sneaking up on anyone or anything. You walk
> like giant buffalos!

She grins and welcomes them in.

> JESSIE, *to William*. You here for another lesson? I'm
> going to give you the names of the animals next.

> WILLIAM. That would be great, but George needs
> to talk with you first.

They all look over to George.

> GEORGE. I got a special delivery letter from Fort
> Russell about Captain Cahill.

Sallie looks away upon hearing his name.

> GEORGE. You know he was very ill the last time I
> went to Fort Russell. In the letter they told me
> that he had died.

There is a gasp from all the women. Sallie gives out a groan, a whimper, and then grabs her belly, which has grown larger these winter months.

> GEORGE. Sallie, I'm sorry. I know you loved him.

> SALLIE. You misunderstand my reactions, George.
> It is one of relief. I might have loved him, but he
> did not love me. When this child comes into the

world, a whole new life for me will begin, one
of unconditional love between a mother and her
child.

JOSIE. We have come together to support Sallie
and her child. There are many children around
this fort that have only their mother due to
battles and disease.

MINIHIE. Together as a family, we will survive.

GEORGE. You know I want to support that. Sallie,
look at me. I love you.

SALLIE. I am sorry to make you wait, but this child
must enter the world first. And I know that
there are many dangers that you face while you
are in the service. Perhaps, when you no longer
have this responsibility, we can be together.

George reaches out for Sallie's hand, and for the first time she lays
her hand on his. Meanwhile, William has been learning some Cheyenne
words with Jessie.

WILLIAM, *to George.* Hey, George, did you know
that the Cheyenne word for spotted tail is
"woostaa"? That is Sallie's Indian name!

GEORGE. I can see my future now, full of William
spouting out Cheyenne Indian words.

Chapter 11

Fort Laramie, June 1868

Sallie is about ready to give birth to her baby. And it happens to coincide with a supply run for William and George. They are around the tepee.

> GEORGE. Look, Sallie, I made a back cradle for
> the baby.

He holds up a beautiful cradle for Sallie to carry her baby on her back.

> SALLIE. I certainly am surprised! Usually, the
> women in the family make such an item.

> GEORGE. Well, I had help from your mother and
> grandmother. They told me what materials I
> needed, and I was able to obtain many of them
> at the Trading Post. Look, I even have moss in
> the bottom!

He opens the lacing on the cradle and shows her the moss at the bottom.

> SALLIE. How nice! Now, when the baby pees and
> poops, I simply remove the moss and put new

moss inside. It is a wonderful gift. Thank you so much!

GEORGE. You're welcome. It was a labor of love.

SALLIE. Speaking of labor, the medicine woman believes that my child will be a daughter. I would be happy to have a girl. She would be the fourth generation for our tepee.

GEORGE. I can't believe women have to go through so much.

SALLIE. It is natural. I am glad to have my mother and grandmother here to help. Some women go into the woods alone and come back with the baby.

WILLIAM. Ouch, that sounds tough. In Iowa we have doctors and midwives.

JOSIE. It is time for you menfolk to leave for a while. Come back in four hours. She is close now.

The women walk into the tepee.

GEORGE, *to William*. I can hardly wait! It's like having my own child, a part of the person I love.

WILLIAM. I have to say it again. You have, like, this really big heart. I really don't think there are many men who would or could accept another man's child as his own.

GEORGE. I have watched this child grow from the very beginning. I have felt it move inside Sallie's belly. I watch her, even now, giving birth.

When they return, Minihie is waiting.

MINIHIE. Come in and see my little granddaughter!

George grabs William by the shoulders.

GEORGE. It's a girl!

He looks over to Minihie.

GEORGE. How is Sallie?

MINIHIE. Tired, but healthy.

George and William walk into the tepee.

GEORGE. Hi, Sallie! Wow, is that your little girl? She is so sweet-looking!

SALLIE. Here, George, you can hold her.

GEORGE. I don't know…

He reaches down and scoops the baby up.

GEORGE. Hello, little beauty.

He looks down at Sallie.

GEORGE. Does she have a name yet?

SALLIE. Yes, it is Lucy.

GEORGE. Hello, little Lucy.

WILLIAM. Can I hold her?

GEORGE. Hold on there, mister. I remember you
    dropping something and almost breaking my
    big toe!

WILLIAM. Don't listen to him, Sallie. I'll be
    careful.

GEORGE. Okay, then.

And with a big, fatherly smile, he hands Lucy over to William. William, says some words in Cheyenne that he hopes means, "Congratulations on the birth of your baby."

JOSIE. Did you just say, "Congratulations on the
    birth of your goat"?

They all start to laugh.

WILLIAM. Oops! Sorry.

Lucy would always be George's firstborn child in his heart and his soul.

Chapter 12

Fort Fetterman, 1870

WILLIAM. George, look over there. I think I see Calamity Jane, a female scout. And isn't that General George Armstrong Custer?

GEORGE. You can't miss him with that fancy outfit of his. If an Indian wanted to kill him, they couldn't miss him.

WILLIAM. That's a terrible thing to say. I did hear that he was responsible for the Washita Massacre.

GEORGE. Sallie and her whole family were traumatized. It was like the Sand Creek Massacre all over again. It just brought back terrible memories. And so many of the casualties were people they knew or family members.

WILLIAM. I hear that Black Kettle, the Southern Cheyenne Peace Chief, was killed with his wife, Medicine Woman Later. They were shot in the back while trying to get away on horseback.

GEORGE. Just like Sand Creek, it was on
  Thanksgiving Day. There was a white flag, but
  they kept shooting.

WILLIAM. Then Custer took over fifty women and
  children as prisoners, and they held them for
  months. It was to force the other tribal members
  to go to a reservation.

GEORGE. Sallie felt she knew what was happening
  to those poor women while they were hostages.

WILLIAM. There is a rumor that Mo-nah-se-
  tah, the daughter of Chief Little Rock, who
  was killed by Custer at Washita, became his
  concubine and bore him a child.

GEORGE. And he's a married man. So much
  for the vows of matrimony. Let's go over and
  meet him."

William looks down at his watch and opens it.

WILLIAM. I think I'll pass. My stomach can't
  handle it.

William walks out of the building, while George goes up and
introduces himself.

Free at Last
George and Sallie's Wedding, 1871

George and William are discharged from the Army at Fort Fetterman
after their three-year enlistment is over.

WILLIAM. So what are you going to do first?

GEORGE. You really need to ask? I'm headed right
over to see Sallie and Lucy.

WILLIAM. You better invite me to the wedding!

GEORGE. Invite you? Why, you're going to be my
best man, aren't you?

WILLIAM. Really? You bet I will.

GEORGE. I already got the wedding band. Let's get
out of this place.

WILLIAM. I'm glad we were able to buy some of
the captured Indian ponies. The saddles were
$10 each, used, but really nice. You ready?

GEORGE. I'm past ready. Bet my horse runs faster
than yours.

WILLIAM. You're on.

They leave through the gates and never look back. George and Sallie
are married at Fort Laramie. William is his best man. Sallie wears a
family heirloom, a beautiful blouse full of elk teeth.

GEORGE, *to Sallie*. Well, how does it feel to be
Mrs. George Harris?

SALLIE. Great! Was I worth waiting for?

GEORGE. You bet. I couldn't be happier.

Lucy comes up with her arms outstretched for George.

LUCY. Papa.

George picks her up and gives her hugs and kisses.

GEORGE. Yes. George is Papa.

SALLIE. My mom and grandma are going to watch
Lucy for us tonight.

She smiles alluringly at George as Minihie comes and takes Lucy from George.

WILLIAM. Well, this is where I leave. I'm renting a
room for the night. Bye!

He rushes off, knowing that they want to be alone.

SALLIE. Come into the tepee with me.

She takes his hand with her hand, the one with her new gold wedding band.

SALLIE. For generations in my family, we have
gotten married the Cheyenne Indian way.

GEORGE. What is the "Cheyenne Indian way"?

Sallie grabs an ornate, colorful blanket from the bed, which is larger than normal. With the blanket around her back and closed in the front by her arms, she approaches George.

SALLIE. In the Cheyenne Indian Way, the woman
chooses the man she will marry. She takes her
blanket around her body and wears it for many
days or months or even years. The man or men
must follow her wherever she goes. He must
help her get food, do nice things for her, and he
must show his bravery. You have done all that

and more for me. When the woman has chosen
which man is worthy of her, the one she wants
to live the rest of her life with, she opens her
blanket and invites her husband to enter.

Sallie opens the blanket, and George enters. She closes the blanket
around them.

GEORGE. Sallie, I will never make you regret your
decision to open your heart and soul to me.

As husband and wife, in both the White man's world and the Indian's
world, George and Sallie conceive their child that night.

Chapter 13

Crazy Woman Creek
Near Trabing, Wyoming Territory, 1871

It is a struggle to make a living in the Wyoming Territory. Most of the country is too harsh for farming, but George has found a way to thrive. With the land he could have from his military service and the money he has saved, he finds a deserted homestead along Crazy Woman Creek. Not far from Trabing, it is an oasis. William comes along, and he helps to build the two-story house, barn, and corrals. There is wood on the property, enough to cut and use for lumber. They dig a well and can pump water inside of the home. The ax and saws see a lot of action. After six months, the land is cleared, the home is built along with a barn, and they have started on the corrals.

> WILLIAM, *hacking down a tree.* I think I have
> lost twenty pounds doing this work! I'm glad
> someone told me to drink lots of water and take
> salt throughout the day, or I would probably be
> dead.

> GEORGE, *hacking down another tree.* You wimp!
> But I have to agree, I have lost twenty pounds
> also.

WILLIAM. But you were much bigger than I was, to start with.

He takes his ax and aims it at George.

WILLIAM. Here, let me take some off with this ax, to even up the score.

GEORGE, *pulling away as he chuckles.* No thanks!

WILLIAM. How are things going with you and Sallie?

GEORGE. She is a wonderful woman, so strong. She is pregnant again.

WILLIAM. Congratulations, George! Pretty soon you should be able to move into the house. That was a nice touch with the water pump inside.

GEORGE. It will come in real handy. Soon we will be setting up the contract with the stagecoach company and we will be setting up the inn. Sallie is such a good cook. She can make something delicious from just about nothing! We will have a horse changing station. The barn will hold the four horses that are exchanged each day. The rest of the land and corrals will be for the cows and sheep.

WILLIAM. What a mix! Don't forget about the chickens too. You have a really nice chicken coop that I made for them.

GEORGE. You are quite handy. You can get the eggs from those chickens without even disturbing them. And for those that don't produce enough eggs, they will be dinner on Sunday.

WILLIAM, *shouting*. Timber!

The little tree he is working on takes a slam into the ground.

GEORGE, *shouting*. Timber!

The next little tree hits the ground.

WILLIAM. Lucky we only need timber for the corrals, as we have just about cut down all the big trees.

GEORGE. You still taking lessons from Jessie?

WILLIAM. Yep. She certainly is growing up into a fine young woman.

GEORGE, *looking at William*. You don't say…

And with a sly grin, he goes after another small tree for timber.

Crazy Woman Creek, Trabing, Wyoming Territory, 1875

GEORGE, *on the porch of their two-story house/inn.* Hey, Sallie, the stage is about to come in. Get ready with the food.

SALLIE. Almost ready! It's a lot harder with three kids, thank you very much. Is William bringing in the supplies today?

GEORGE. Yep!

SALLIE. How about the wood for the stove and
    fireplace? I only have enough for one more day.

GEORGE. I'll go see if Albert is working on it.

George gets up from the porch and goes to the barn to be sure the horses for the exchange will be ready for the stagecoach. He looks around the corner of the barn and can see that Alban "Albert" Dumont Spang is there. Albert had been born in San Francisco, right after the beginning of the gold rush in California. He had been born into the West and was always eager for a new challenge.

GEORGE. I see you are hard at work. I really
    appreciate that.

ALBERT. Well, it's easy to work for a man who
    treats me like family.

He lifts up the ax and splices another piece of log for firewood.

ALBERT. Charles Powell will be joining me in
    a few days to help collect the wood and in
    cutting it.

GEORGE. We want to have plenty of wood for the
    wintertime. I hear something coming. It might
    be the stage.

George heads back toward the inn. Sallie is already at the doorway. But it is not the stage. It is William with the supplies.

GEORGE. I didn't expect you for another few
    hours. You'll have to pull the wagon over by the
    side as the stagecoach is coming.

WILLIAM. It's just like the old days. I know where
all the chuckholes are.

They both chuckle. William positions the wagonful of supplies by the side of the inn. Then they hear the real thing come. Four powerful horses pulling a stagecoach. Sometimes it is just one or two passengers, but today there are six people crammed in along with two drivers. The luggage rack is full.

GEORGE, *to the stagecoach driver*. Hi, Cal! How
was the ride so far? Any troubles?

CAL.. I thought I saw a Cheyenne warrior, but he
did not seem to want anything from us.

Cal suddenly looks upward and sniffs the air.

CAL. I smell something delicious. Did Sallie fix my
favorite stew?

SALLIE, *walking out of the front door*. You sure
have a good sniffer. Hurry on in, people. Nice
to meet you all. Looks like it was a dusty ride.
Go on in the powder room to the right. The
outhouse is in the back.

The six passengers get out of the stage, including a young girl about five years old. Some can get out easier than others. The men try to help the women out and down to the ground. George recognizes two of them.

GEORGE. Well, lookee here, is that Wild Bill
Hickock and Calamity Jane?

WILD BILL, turning to see George. Wow, is
that George? It's been a long time since Fort
Fetterman! Calamity and I are headed to

Deadwood. I hear it's just ripe for the taking with all that new gold in the Black Hills.

CALAMITY JANE. Well, I can see that you and Sallie are doing great. How many children you got?

GEORGE. Three now. My eldest, Lucy, she's at school. The rest you'll meet inside. Hurry on in and Sallie will serve up some of her delicious stew.

WILLIAM, *to George.* You see that outfit that Wild Bill has on? With the black hat, silver work on the band, leather belt, and black vest, black pants, and boots? Someday I am going to have an outfit just like that. I'm sure ready for some really good food. Where's Albert?

GEORGE. Behind the barn, chopping wood.

WILLIAM. I'll go get him.

William runs over to the barn.

WILLIAM. Hey, Albert, time to stop work for a while. Dinner's ready!

ALBERT. You got back already? Did you get what I needed for the wood?

WILLIAM. Sure, I did. And it's a beauty of a chisel. Now you can really break up the wood.

ALBERT. I'm going to have a partner to help me
get wood and chop it up. His name is Charles
Powell. He should be here any day.

WILLIAM. Glad you are getting help. Wood is
so important for the inn. We couldn't survive
without it. Let's get going. I'm starved!

Albert places the ax against the barn, and they both run to the house.
They are the last two to be seated. Along with the passengers, there are
the two children of Sallie and George.

SALLIE, *to a couple with child.* How old is your
little girl?

MR. COLBY. She is five years old.

SALLIE. What is her name?

MRS. COLBY. Daisy.

Immediately, and without hesitation, Sallie and George's youngest
son, William G, speaks up.

WILLIAM G.Daisy? Auck! Why, that's the name
for a cow!

George loses it and spews out food from his mouth. And then he
begins to laugh, without control. Sallie is so embarrassed she doesn't
know what to say.

WILLIAM. Why, Daisy is a very nice name. Daisies
are so sweet. I bet you're just like them.

The face on Daisy goes from one of anger to a smile, and everything
returns to normal.

Chapter 14

Stagecoach Stop and Inn
Trabing, Wyoming Territory, 1875

Tensions all over Wyoming, Nebraska, Kansas, Oklahoma, Colorado, Montana, and the Dakotas are now very high. What is being called the Indian Wars is at its peak. Raids on farms have the White people scared, and Indian tribes have to constantly move. Even nonhostile tribes know they are not safe. The inn at Trabing never has any raids, perhaps because Sallie lives there.

It is spring, and Sallie's family is going to move from Fort Laramie to her home. It really isn't safe for them there anymore; too much racial discrimination. It is a Sunday, the only day there are no stages to tend to. George and Sallie are on the porch.

> SALLIE. I'm looking forward to seeing my mom,
> sister, and grandmother. And they get to see our
> babies. They can help me with the chores and
> with the kids.

> GEORGE. You know I am okay with this. I want
> them to be safe, and most of your relatives have
> moved or have joined the Sioux. I've always
> hoped they would agree to come join us.

SALLIE. I'm glad William was able to see them
    once a month when he went in for supplies. He
    certainly learned Cheyenne. Jessie has been a
    good teacher.

GEORGE. William started out early yesterday
    morning. He wanted to get into Fort Laramie to
    pack up their items and get them back here.

SALLIE. I know, I have to be patient. Wait, do I
    hear them?

She runs down the porch steps to get a better look down the road.
She can see the dust, and then the wagon. William pulls up to the front
of the inn and pulls the brake on the wagon.

WILLIAM. Okay, we're here!

HUMPBACK WOMAN/ JOSIE, *sitting next to
    William.* It is such a wonderful home. And it is
    so nice to see Sallie.

Sallie is jumping up and down with joy, which is hard to do because
she is pregnant again. Her three children come out of the door.

MINIHIE. Oh look, Jessie, look! Babies, my
    grandbabies!

William has jumped down from the wagon seat and has walked
around to the wagon gate. He unlatches it so that Minihie and Jessie
can get out. They have to be careful as their belongings are also there.
He then walks around to Josie to help her down from the wagon. Sallie
runs over to Jessie and grabs her by the shoulders.

SALLIE. You are so grown-up. I can't believe how
    mature you look.

JESSIE. I hope we are never apart this long ever
again. I have missed you a lot.

She looks down at the children at her feet.

JESSIE. So which one is this hanging on my dress?

Sallie points to each one as she calls out their names.

SALLIE. Mom, sis, and Grandma, this is Julia,
Elizabeth, and William G. And as you can tell, I
am going to have another one!

MINIHIE. My sweet daughter, how wonderful to
see so many children!

JESSIE. This is so wonderful. I'm so glad we can
stay here and help you!

SALLIE. Me too!

William and George help to get up the tepee in the backyard, which
is a little worse for wear after all these years.

JOSIE. I have lived in a tepee all my life, and I don't
think I will change now.

MINIHIE. Me too. But we will be close by now, so
you can call on us for help.

William walks up to Jessie and talks to her in Cheyenne. By her
looks, you could tell she likes what he has to say.

WILLIAM. George and Sallie, I have been hiding a
secret from you. We didn't want to tell you until

we were all together. I asked Jessie to marry me,
and she accepted!

Sallie shouts with happiness and claps her hands. George walks up
to William.

> GEORGE. Congratulations, William. I guess that
> means we are now related. It couldn't have
> happened to a better set of friends.

He slaps William on the back, hard enough for William to flinch.
Sallie runs up to Jessie to give her a hug. Minihie and Josie are looking
at one of the best times in their lives.

> JOSIE, to *Minihie*. After so much pain and
> suffering, we can look at our family and be so
> grateful to Ma'heo'o, our Great Spirit.

> MINIHIE. Mom, it has really been your strength
> and courage that has gotten us through. You
> were the one that knew how to save us at Sand
> Creek. We wouldn't be here without your
> strength and guidance.

> JOSIE. It is wonderful to see children that are
> happy and safe. It has been far too long.

Two Months Later

The wedding of William and Jessie goes as planned. Of course,
George is best man, and Sallie was the matron of honor. Jessie wears the
families elk tooth blouse. They have tables of food and drink.

At the end of the day, William and Jessie are alone together. They
walk to the room that would be their home while they live with George
and Sallie. Jessie has her family's colorful blanket on the bed.

WILLIAM. I think I remember George telling me
about this blanket. Is that the same one?

JESSIE. I, too, would like to have a White man's
wedding and an Indian wedding. Please leave
the room for a few minutes and then come
back.

William leaves the room and looks at his watch. It is early yet. He
has been waiting for so many years for Jessie. She was so young when he
met her, and now she is his wife. As he closes the watch, he could hear
Jessie beckoning him into the room. He walks in and closes the door.

WILLIAM. I am here, but it is so dark.

JESSIE. All the better.

He can hear noises as she comes closer. He can feel her presence,
the opening of the blanket. He walks in; his desire for her is so great.
William is thrilled to feel that she is naked and he can feel her like he
has always wanted to feel her. They stand in that moment for a while,
realizing that each would give to the other their heart and soul.

WILLIAM. I will love you forever.

JESSIE, *stating something in Cheyenne, then in
English.* Me too, my dear William, now and
forever, in this life and the next.

As they slip onto the bed, William struggles to get his clothes off.
When he does, he could feel the body of his wife and she could feel his.
Like Sallie and George before them, they conceive their child that night.

Custer's Last Stand, June 1876

It is a horrible event, and yet most people know it would happen. General George Armstrong Custer is killed at the Little Big Horn. Stories about the battle begin to trickle in from the travelers along the road. Eventually, Jessie's family pieces together who have been in the battle. Some of their own family members have been there. Some have died. The survivors in the tribes think the battle is a glorious conquest, but it is the beginning of the end for "free" Indians. George and William know the danger their wives and children would face.

WILLIAM. I just found out that Jessie is pregnant.

GEORGE. That's wonderful! Now you get to know
what my life is like. Sallie is just about to give
birth to our fourth baby!

WILLIAM. How does it feel to be a dad?

GEORGE. Wonderful and terrifying. You suddenly
become responsible for this little bundle of
joy. That little person is so dependent on you
to provide it shelter and food it can make you
sweat!

WILLIAM. I'm looking forward to it. I wonder
who this child will look like?

GEORGE. Well, I hope it doesn't get your ears!

WILLIAM. Oh, hush. My daughter would look
great with my ears.

They both chuckles.

WILLIAM. Will we be able to protect our wives and
our children? After Custer's death, the public's
perception of the Indian has gone to hell.

GEORGE. Luckily, we aren't in a big city. There
is just us and the stage that comes through.
Perhaps it will all calm down after a while.

WILLIAM. I get a feeling that it will take
generations.

GEORGE. I always knew those fancy clothes would
get Custer into trouble.

WILLIAM. I heard Jessie talking to Sallie.
Apparently, Custer wasn't mutilated like the rest.
He had a needle shoved into each ear and an
arrow shoved up his penis.

GEORGE. Gruesome! I guess I'm glad he was dead
for that last one. Why do you think they did
that?

WILLIAM. I heard Jessie say it was because at one
of the treaty meetings, he signed a document
with the Cheyenne. At the meeting, he made
a promise never to fight the Cheyenne. The
women put the needles in his ears to open them
up so he could hear his promise.

GEORGE. And the arrow?

WILLIAM. That was because he took the daughter
of Chief Little Rock as his hostage and then had
a son with her.

GEORGE. Well, it does sound kind of logical. But
the negative feelings toward Indians are not
going to be good for us.

Chapter 15

Trabing, Wyoming, 1880

Cattle barons have a huge number of cattle that are using free public ranges. Small cattle ranchers are starting to attend cattle roundups, where they begin taking deserted or orphaned calves and branding them for their ranch.

> GEORGE. You know, William, we just keep adding mouths at our table. The inn and stagecoach are not enough. We need to do something else to raise money.
>
> WILLIAM. What do you have in mind?
>
> GEORGE. We need to start a cattle ranch.
>
> WILLIAM. Huh? What do we know about cattle or how to raise them or how to sell them? How would we even afford to buy one to get started?
>
> GEORGE. Aw, that's the whole idea. When the large ranchers have their roundups in the spring, we will go out with them and take in all the orphaned calves.

WILLIAM. Isn't that stealing?

GEORGE. Nah. The calves would die without their
        mother. We would get a cow that produces milk
        and take in all the strays. They can feed off the
        one cow. When they get bigger, we keep the
        cows for their milk and sell the bulls or steers.
        We might get so big we could keep a bull and
        breed it to our cows!

WILLIAM. Gee, that just might work. We would
        have to get the first cow and patent a branding
        iron.

GEORGE. You know more than you are willing
        to say.

That spring, everyone leaves the inn to cull the orphan calves off the
free range. They find ten the first year, fifteen the next, and soon they
have forty cattle and are selling thirty-five of them each year.

George's Stagecoach Inn, Wyoming Territory, 1881

Lucy is coming home from the Indian Boarding School, and everyone
is excited.

SALLIE. Oh, George, it has been so long since we
        have seen her. You think we will recognize her?

GEORGE. Of course we will! I bet she looks as
        beautiful as you do.

George grabs her chin softly and gives her a kiss. She smiles and
acknowledges his act of love with a smile.

SALLIE. I was so scared for her, being there alone. But they said that would be better for her, to keep her in the White man's world. Luckily, she didn't get any of those diseases that have killed so many of our Indian children.

GEORGE. Our little girl is all grown up. I think that's the stagecoach now. With the train so popular now, I wonder how long this stop will last.

The stage stops, and there is only one passenger. It is Lucy.

SALLIE. Oh, my dear, my child, I have missed you so much!

Tears come to her eyes. George helps her out, and Sallie grabs Lucy. Lucy is now crying, also in her arms.

LUCY. And I have missed you!

George is standing aside, watching the reunion. Lucy turns and sees George.

LUCY. Oh, Papa, I am so glad to see you too!

She runs up and gives him a hug, and he gives her one right back.

GEORGE. You look spectacular! Did they treat you okay?

LUCY. It is a different world, and they wanted me to forget everything I had learned as a child. My Cheyenne language was never to be spoken. I had to change the way I wore my hair. I had to

eat different foods. Even the games I played had
to be different. The Indian way was thrown out.

LUCY. (she says something in Cheyenne) Yeah! I
can still remember!

William and Jessie come out together.

LUCY. Aunt Jessie, Uncle William. I heard you are
going to have another child. Congratulations!

WILLIAM. We are so happy to see you! I can't help
but remember the day you were born. Everyone
was afraid I was going to drop you!

They all laugh. Albert has just come around the corner of the house.
He had been at the barn cutting wood, as usual. His reaction is immediate.
He walks right up to Lucy.

ALBERT. Hellooooooo! My name is Albert, and
who is this beautiful young lady?

He bows and takes her hand and kisses it.

LUCY. My, my, my, aren't you the gentleman! I am
Lucy, George and Sallie's daughter.

ALBERT. What! How can that be? I was told that
you were but a child, but you are a lovely,
mature young woman! We must get to know
each other.

George and William are rolling their eyes. Jessie and Sallie are
giggling at how ridiculous it sounds. But it turns out to be the beginning
of a sweet romance.

Canyon Ranch, Crazy Women's Creek,
Near Buffalo, Johnson County, Wyoming Territory,
Christmas Day, December 25, 1885

On Christmas Day 1885 at Canyon Ranch, Crazy Women's Creek, near Buffalo, Wyoming Territory, Alban "Albert" Dumont Spang and Lucy (Cahill) Harris became man and wife.

> WILLIAM. Welcome to the family, Albert. I thought one day this would happen. Now we are the three musketeers.

> GEORGE. You better be good to that little daughter of mine, or I'll come after you! You know how hard I can hit with my knuckles!

He holds up his fist.

> ALBERT. I sure do.

Albert backs away as Lucy comes up and throws her arm against his chest.

> LUCY. Don't worry, Albert. I'll protect you.

Chapter 16

Johnson County Cattle Wars, Wyoming Territory
Summer 1886

The three families work hard together. Children are born. Together George and Sallie continue to run the stagecoach and inn. Jessie and Lucy are there to help, while Minihie and Josie help to watch all the children. Sometimes the little girls want to be Indian maidens or pioneer girls. Sometimes the little boys want to be braves or cowboys. Each spring they all leave for the spring roundup and stray calves would be brought home. They have a chuck wagon run by the women, while the men go out to rope the calves and brand them. It is a good life and a good living, but times are changing. It starts with the summer of 1886. George, William, and Albert are sitting in chairs on the porch of the inn.

> GEORGE, *to William*. It's a really hot summer.
> Things are drying up so quickly.
>
> WILLIAM. I know. I'm kind of worried. Even if we
> cut some grass for feed, like we have done in the
> past, it is so dry it won't feed the stock we have.
>
> ALBERT. I hate to think what will happen if the
> winter is a bad one.
>
> GEORGE. Jeez, Albert, don't jinx us!

Lucy comes up with a platter full of glasses.

LUCY. You want some lemonade?

ALL THE MEN, *together*. You bet!

In runs Benjamin, William's boy. He runs up to his dad.

WILLIAM. Hey, Ben, what's wrong? Why aren't
you playing with the others?

BENJAMIN. I was playing Indian and George was
playing Custer, and he said he shot me dead.
But I told him it was the other way around: I
shot him dead.

For a moment, William is not sure what to say, and George and
Albert are looking at William to see what he has to say.

WILLIAM. Well, you know what, Ben? If people
keep on fighting, then both will die. But if you
try to live without violence, then you both can
live.

BEN. Hmmm, so I need to make a treaty?

WILLIAM. Yes, but, and this is important, the
treaty must be honest and truthful, and both
sides need to agree. There should be no threats
on either side, and it should make both sides
happy with the results. You need someone that
can help you do this. Pick one of the girls.

BEN. What? I have to play with the girls?

WILLIAM. I suspect when you get older, you will
want to play with girls.

All the adults laugh.

BEN. Urgh, Dad! Okay, I'll do it. I'll go ask Mary
Gertrude. Thanks, Dad!

Ben leaves and goes to find the others playing in the backyard.

GEORGE, *to Lucy*. Great lemonade.

LUCY. Thanks, Pa!

LUCY, *to Alban*. Oh, and by the way, I'm pregnant
again.

Albert jumps up and grabs her.

ALBERT. Yahoo!

WILLIAM, *to George*. He's a chip off the same
block.

Trabing, Wyoming Territory, Winter 1886

The winter of 1886 is one of the worst on record. The cattle barons
are hit the hardest. Their cattle depend on the open range, but there is
nothing they could find to eat. The drifts are high and bury them. It is
so cold their hooves freeze to the ground. Even William, George, and
Alban lose some cattle, but many more survive because they have feed
in the barn that they could distribute. Unlike some farmers that have
only cattle, they also have sheep. Because of their wool, they do not die
off. The men are huddled around the inn's fireplace.

GEORGE, *to William and Albert.* That was the
worst winter on record. I've never seen such
high drifts and cold ground. The cattle froze
in the drifts, starved, or couldn't even move
because their hooves were frozen to the ground.

WILLIAM. We're lucky we had some feed for the
animals, or more of them would have died.

ALBERT. It looks like the sheep did better than the
cattle. Maybe we ought to raise more sheep.

GEORGE. Well, I know it is not done by most,
but why can't we do both? This is going to be a
sad year during the spring roundup. I think we
should not even attempt one.

WILLIAM. I'm in agreement: no use wasting our
time.

ALBERT. The cattle barons are getting together and
fencing off their land. They have strung barbed
wire all over. It is such nasty stuff.

GEORGE. People who have been saving orphaned
calves are now being looked at like cattle thieves.
Laws are changing so that getting a patent on
a branding iron is severely restricted. I heard
from one of our friends that their water supply
has been cut off by a cattle baron farther up the
stream.

WILLIAM. I am seeing more and more laws that
are supporting the cattle barons ahead of us
small cattle ranchers. It is harder to get justice.
I'm thinking there is some bribing going on

and all the lawmen and judges are paid by the
barons.

ALBERT. It doesn't seem right. Something should
be done.

George Harris Ranch, Trabing, Wyoming, 1887

Because the winter has been so harsh, George finds himself in
debt. He decides that he would need to sell some of his horses. He has
seventy-six mares and geldings that he auctions off. The man that buys
them is the foreman of the 76 Ranch, Fred Hesse. He works for the
cattle barons. Although he receives only $2,000 per year in wages as a
foreman, he has a large ranch house with all the new farming equipment
and a large tract of land that is fenced in. One has to wonder where he
gets his extra income.

GEORGE, *to William and Albert.* I just finished
the books, and we are not going to make it this
spring and summer. Our expenses are going to
be way over our income, and I already owe some
money to the bank for some wood I had to
buy. If we don't come up with some income, we
might lose the inn.

WILLIAM. Maybe Albert and I can go out and
earn some extra income helping other farmers
nearby?

GEORGE. It won't be enough. I think we need to
sell most of our horses. We can keep the hardier,
stronger ones for the stage. And I wouldn't want
to sell our personal riding horses. My children,
and yours, William, have some ponies that I can
make sure are not sold. I know how much those

ponies mean to the kids. That would be about fifteen. We have ninety-one horses, so we can sell seventy-six, which are mostly range mares and geldings.

ALBERT. Well, I'll help you gather them up.

WILLIAM. Me too.

GEORGE. I'll set up an auction for their sale to the highest bidder.

Auction, One Month Later

William, *to George.* Albert and I did our best, but six of those horses were very elusive. We have seen them and know they are out there, but we had problems getting a rope over their heads to bring them in. I'm afraid we only have seventy horses here. What do you want to do?

GEORGE. I'll go ahead and sell the seventy-six horses, and we will get the six out of the range as soon as we can. Wait, I think I hear the auctioneer now.

At the end of the auction, Fred Hesse has bought all seventy-six of the horses.

GEORGE, to *Fred Hesse.* Well, I see that you have purchased all the horses that I had for auction. You will notice that only seventy of them are here at the moment. The other six are out in the range, and I will have to locate them and bring them to you. It might take a few weeks.

FRED HESSE. I want to have them right away. Certainly, you have not sold all your horses here.

GEORGE. No, I still have some at H. W. Devoe's
pasture. About fifteen head. But these are the
horses that belong to me, my household, and
my children. They are not animals that I wish
to sell. I am good on my word, but if you are
worried, we can sign a contract guaranteeing
that you will get the other six horses.

FRED. Okay, let's sign a contract.

The Next Morning

Fred knows that better horses are at Devoe's and sends two men to
take the six from this pasture.

FRED, *to two employees*. I want the two of you to go
over to Devoe's pasture and get the fifteen horses
you find there with George Harris's brand. Take
six of them and place my brand on them. I have
a right to them.

FIRST EMPLOYEE. Sure, boss, we can do that.

They mount their horses and set out to Devoe's ranch. When they
get there, they find the pasture with George Harris's horses and start
to set them free.

H. W. DEVOE, *to Joe, a hired hand*. Look, out in
the pasture. Who is that setting the horses free?
I did not order that. It must be Fred Hesse and
his gang. I saw George and him having some
discussion over the last six horses. Joe, get your
horse and get over to George's ranch right away.
He needs to come here and stop these men!

Joe gets on his horse and gallops as fast as he can to George's ranch.

JOE. George…George, come out here quickly!

George runs out of the inn.

JOE. Mr. Devoe says that some men are taking your
horses out of his pasture. He needs you right
away.

GEORGE. I'm getting my horse now. Do you think
it is the work of Fred Hesse?

JOE. Yes.

GEORGE. That goddamn son of a gun!

George mounts his horse, with his rifle and handguns, and gallops
with Joe back to Devoe's ranch. When he gets there, his horses are
running throughout the area. He knows where to find six of them, at
Fred's ranch. He heads out there. He rides up to the fancy ranch house.

GEORGE. Hey, Fred, come out here!

Fred comes out.

GEORGE. Mr. Devoe states that some of your men
came over to his pasture and let my horses out
of his pasture. What is going on?

FRED. I don't know what you are talking about. I
had two of my employees go out in the range
and find six of your horses. I thought I would
help you locate them. They are in the corral in
the back, already branded.

George rides his horse over to the back corral and sees six of his horses that have previously been in Devoe's pasture. One of them belongs to his daughter Julia, and another one belongs to his son William G. A third one is owned by his friend William. He dismounts and goes up to them.

GEORGE. Hi, Princess. Come here, girl.

Princess comes up.

GEORGE. I'm so sorry this is happening to you.
Julia will miss you.

He calls another horse.

GEORGE. Here, Buster. Come here, boy.

The black horse comes up.

GEORGE. Hi, Buster. I'm going to miss you the
most. William G is going to miss you a lot also.
He took such good care of you and enjoyed
riding you.

He calls to another horse.

GEORGE. Here, Apple.

An appaloosa comes prancing up and then rubs the dirt with one hoof.

GEORGE. William certainly loved your spirit. I
hope you buck your riders off. Give them hell!

George got back up on his horse and rode back.

GEORGE. You know, Fred, this is bad dealings.
     These horses were not for sale, and I believe you
     knew where they came from.

FRED. Well, George, I would say you just need to
     call this transaction completed and head back
     home.

George hears some guns being readied for discharge. He turns and sees the two employees with their pistols aimed at him, cocked and ready to shoot.

GEORGE. You might get away with this now, but
     someday in the future, you will get what you
     deserve.

George returns to his ranch and has the sad task of telling his children and his friend about what happened. It is a story that travels throughout Johnson County.

Chapter 17

George's Inn, Crazy Creek, Wyoming Territory
July 21, 1889

Albert rides in with his horse to the inn, gets off, and ties him up. He then runs into the home.

ALBERT. William, George, come quick.

William and George come rushing in from different areas of the home.

ALBERT. I just came back from Trabing. James
Averell and Ella Watson were lynched for cattle
rustling yesterday. They were hanged, and
they're dead!

WILLIAM. What! No! My God, what is this world
coming to? James didn't even own cattle, and
Ella only owned about twenty-five.

GEORGE. I think the real conflict was over
their land. The barons wanted their land for
right-of-way.

WILLIAM. Now we have something to worry
about. This is going to affect everyone.

ALBERT. There is going to be a meeting, a secret
     meeting, for all the small cattle ranchers. It's
     going to be at Nate Champion's ranch. I think
     we ought to go.

GEORGE. I think only one of us should go. If
     there are any spies at the meeting, then they will
     think that only one of us is involved. I'll go.

WILLIAM. No, I should go.

GEORGE. No, I should go. It was my suggestion
     all those years ago to get into ranching after all.

ALBERT. Okay, George, but you know that
     whatever you decide, William and I are right
     behind you.

GEORGE. Okay.

One Week Later

On the designated day, during the dark of night, the small ranchers
come together. The head speaker is already talking when George arrives.
He could see their shadows through the windowpanes. Many horses are
posted around the area. His horse snorts as he gets off and ties him up.
Behind a tree higher up on the hillside in the forest stands a lone man
with a telescope, spying on those who have gone in. He is keeping a list
of men that he knows are there to "cause trouble."

George opens the door and walks in. The air is full of cigarette and
cigar smoke. At a table at the front of the meeting is a vibrant, handsome
cowboy. His voice is loud, and he is well-spoken.

NATHANIEL CHAMPION (NATE). This has
     to stop. We are being murdered unfairly! I'm

against rustling, just like the barons are. But
to take innocent citizens, arrest them, and
then allow them to be lynched? Well, that
just cannot happen again. We cannot let that
happen again. Only by coming together can
we have any chance against the Wyoming
Stock Growers Association. We need to form
our own association. I propose that the name
be the Northern Wyoming Farmers and Stock
Growers' Association.

There are "Yesses," and "Yahoos," and "Ya betchas" throughout the crowd.

> NATE. Let's do it, then. I had these papers created
> with all the legal stuff. We just need to sign
> them.

A rush of people starts to get up when George pipes up.

> GEORGE. Nate, sorry to interrupt, but how are
> we going to protect ourselves and our families?
> I propose that a fund be set up to care for any
> widows and children that are affected by this.
> We all should chip in.

> NATE. Your name?

> GEORGE. George Harris.

> NATE. You're the gentleman that owns the stage
> stop on Crazy Woman's Creek.

> GEORGE. Yes.

> NATE. I think that is a great idea.

GEORGE. And I think we need to get together
    some law enforcers that will protect us. I suggest
    that we approach Sheriff Angus Red.

NATE. You've got some really great ideas. Can you
    stay after the meeting to help us figure out how
    to carry out these ideas?

GEORGE. Yes.

NATE. Any others want to stay? Raise your hands.
    I see five others. Please stay. Okay, come up
    and sign this form so we can start our new
    association.

There is a big rush as the people sign up. As they walk out, you can
hear their horses leave. The five men plus George and Nate are left to
discuss the details.

GEORGE. I think each member of our association
    needs to contribute $10 for the wives and
    children's fund.

NATE. According to this form, fifty-two members
    have signed. That would make $520.

MEMBER RUSTY. I hate to think of this, but it
    might have to be split for more than one widow.

NATE. We are all worried about the outcome. The
    barons are powerful. They have purchased lots
    of land in order to close off public grazing lands.

MEMBER GABE. Land that we have a right to!

Gabe slams his hand on the table.

NATE. I know, Gabe. It's not fair. We also know that many creeks and streams are being cut off farther up their source by the barons.

MEMBER ZACH. That was what happened to me. Luckily, I knew how to dig a well and use a windmill to get the water up, or my cattle would be dead by now.

NATE. That would be a handy thing to teach the other farmers so that they can survive their water being cut off. We should send you out to the farms that are being affected by this. Are you willing to help them? Are you willing to go out to their farms and show them how?

ZACH. You bet ya!

NATE. We need to make sure we are strong with the law as well. I think most of the sheriffs and judges have been bought off, but I also believe that Sheriff Red Angus is an honest man and that he will support us.

GEORGE. Nate, do you have men around you that you can trust to protect you? Once the barons find out that you have organized the small ranchers, your life won't be worth two cents. I think we all want you to be around a long time.

NATE. Luckily, the men on my ranch are honest, hardworking, and good shots. Well, we have a lot of organizing. I'll turn in our papers for the association tomorrow.

George leaves Nate's home. It is very late. When he gets home, Sallie is still awake.

SALLIE. Oh, George. I was so worried for you!

Tears are coming to her eyes.

SALLIE. What would I do without you? What would the children do without you?

GEORGE. Don't worry, honey. I don't plan on dying on you. But as a community, we have to come together or we may as well let the barons take over our land right now. It is worth fighting for. Our life here is worth fighting for. Our friends and family are worth fighting for!

SALLIE. I am so proud of you, and I am so proud to be your wife.

GEORGE. I'm glad I have your support, and I'm proud to be your husband.

He puts his arm around her, and they walk to their bedroom.

Chapter 18

Wyoming, Several Years Later

In 1890, Wyoming becomes an official State. George, William, and Albert continue to work with the other ranchers to get justice for their cause. The barons start to pay off the train masters so they would only take cattle from the barons to market. And then the worst insult, they hire fifty gunmen from Texas. Some of them are notorious gangsters. Some are mercenaries. Some are ex-Texas Rangers. All of them have their guns aimed at the small ranchers. There is a list of men they are hired to serve warrants to, but there are no warrants. It really is a list of those that the barons want dead. At the top of the list is Nate Champion, President of the Northern Wyoming Farmers and Stock Growers' Association. On the way from Texas, once they get into Wyoming, they cut the telegraph lines so that there could be no calls for help. They start to head to Buffalo, where they think they would get some additional men to support their murderous goals, but decide to stop at the KC Ranch, where Nate Champion is renting land for his two hundred head of cattle. One attempt on his life has already been made, but he has escaped. Now with so many men, they know he would not escape again.

*The Ranch of Oscar Hite "Jack" Flagg
and his Wife, Maria "Imogene" (Spang/Taylor)
April 9, 1892*

Oscar Hite "Jack" Flagg is talking to his eldest stepson, Alonzo Taylor (seventeen years old).

> JACK. Well, it looks like we have the extra wood
> and posts in the wagon for your uncle Albert.
> He's waiting in Trabing for us. He says he is
> bringing his friends George and William. They
> run the stagecoach and inn nearby. We'll be
> traveling through Nate's property on the KC
> Ranch as a shortcut. How are the hitches on
> those two horses? Did you secure the wood? I
> don't want any to slip out.

> ALONZO. Everything is fine, Jack. You worry too
> much. Mom wants me back for dinner, so we
> better get going. I've got the rifle in the back,
> just in case we see some game on the way.

Jack pulls his horse out, and Alonzo slaps the reins for the two horses to start pulling the wagon. After a few miles, they reach the hillside looking down on the KC Ranch. They can see the barn and the house. Jack needs to make a stop at the woods.

> JACK, *to Alonzo.* You see the barn down the hill and
> the bridge after that? Go directly over the bridge
> and head to the right. I have to make a quick
> stop into the woods here.

Jack dismounts his horse and makes it into the woods. Alonzo makes a slow route toward the barn. He is then stopped by a stranger on foot, dressed in black, with a rough, unshaven face. He has run out from behind the barn with a repeating rifle in his hand.

STRANGER. Stop! Get down from the wagon!

The stranger reaches for the reins of the horses, but Alonzo has no intention of stopping and starts to slap his horses with their reins so that they lurch toward the bridge. The stranger raises his rifle and shoots. He misses. The horses startle and start to run, in a frenzy, over the bridge. In the meantime, Jack has started back down the hillside and sees what is happening to Alonzo. He removes his handgun from the holster and shoots at the stranger, who retreats back to behind the barn. But there are others near the gully by the bridge and along the road. The man in the gully attempts to shoot Alonzo in the wagon but misses, hitting the backboard instead. As Jack comes through, he shoots at the man in the gully, who ducks down. Other men have started to shoot. Jack slips down his saddle to the right side of his horse so that the bullets cannot hit him. Jack has now caught up with Alonzo, who throws him the rifle from the back of the wagon. They slow down and fire back at some horsemen that are coming their way. A horse falls, and another man picks up the fallen man, and they head back to the barn. More horsemen are coming.

> JACK, *to Alonzo*. I think Nate is in big trouble. Last
> fall, there was an attempt on his life. These men
> must be trying to kill him. I need you to cut
> the horses free from the wagon, mount the best
> runner, and let's get out of here.

> ALONZO. Geez, they almost got me, twice!

> JACK. I know. I'm sure glad they missed you. Your
> mother would have never forgiven me.

They look at each other, and they both laugh. Alonzo cuts free the horses from the wagon, and he mounts the best runner. They head as fast as they can toward Trabing. Little do they know that their wagon would be dragged back to the ranch and used as a torch to burn down the ranch house.

As they approach Trabing, Jack heads toward Albert. William and George are there as well.

> ALBERT, *to William and George.* Look, guys, I can
> see Jack coming into town. This does not look
> good. There is no wagon, and Alonzo is on a
> horse with no saddle. Wow, Jack, you look like
> people are after you. What's happening? Where's
> the wagon? You okay, Alonzo?

> ALONZO. I'm okay, Uncle Albert. But you won't
> believe what we have been through…

> JACK. Alonzo, you need to head back home. Let
> your mom know what is happening, and get
> the guns loaded in case those men recognized us
> and want to keep us from talking. Take the long
> way around.

> ALONZO. Okay, I'm headed out. Be careful, Jack.

Alonzo pulls on the reins to get oriented back home. He sees the second horse coming into town, runs him down, grabs the reins, and takes the horse with him. Jack looks over at him.

> JACK. He's a good boy…

He looks back at Albert.

> JACK. Albert, I had to abandon our wagon with the
> wood I promised you. Alonzo and I almost got

killed by some strangers. There is a shoot-out at the KC Ranch. I think there are men trying to kill Nate Champion. He doesn't have a chance unless we get some men there. Can you come with me?

ALBERT. You can count me in.

GEORGE AND WILLIAM, together. Me too.

They all mount their horses and head toward the KC Ranch. On their way, they meet twelve other men with Sheriff Red Angus, who has been alerted by a next-door neighbor of the KC Ranch, Terrance Smith. He knows there must be trouble when he hears gunfire.

> JACK. Boy, am I glad to see you, Sheriff! We were just headed back to the KC Ranch. This is my brother-in-law Albert Spang, and his coworkers, William Bixby and George Harris. I was just at the KC Ranch and saw firsthand what is happening there. There are at least ten men there, maybe more, and they have the cabin surrounded. My guess is that Nate is inside. He doesn't stand a chance without us.

> SHERIFF ANGUS. Nate's neighbor Terrance Smith heard gunfire at the KC and realized that there must be trouble. We got as many men as we could get at such a late hour. Are you the George Harris that runs the stage stop and inn?

> GEORGE. Yes, I am. I know Nate from the Cattle Association meetings. If what Jack has told us is true, then there are quite a few men trying to kill Nate as we speak.

They all gallop to just outside of the KC Ranch. The fifty murderers are just leaving.

> SHERIFF. Look, they are leaving! We can set up
> an ambush. You seven go into the ditch side to
> the left, and you seven head up to the top of the
> hillside road. When they make this sharp turn,
> we will jump out and they will surrender, or die.

So, they set up an ambush. But one of the men shot his gun off too early and the murderers turn around and take a different route.

> SHERIFF. Dang it, Jonathan, you shooting off your
> gun did not help at all! Except now they don't
> have a quick route to Buffalo.
>
> JONATHAN. Sorry, Sheriff. It was so hard to see. I
> thought I saw them, but it must have been some
> animal.
>
> SHERIFF. I need a volunteer to follow them and to
> tell me where they camp for the night.

Jack raises his hand.

> SHERIFF. Okay, Jack, come back when you know
> where they are headed. After we go and look at
> the KC Ranch, I am going to head to Buffalo
> and get some more volunteers.

Disappointed that the ambush failed, the posse goes to the KC Ranch. What they see is sickening.

> SHERIFF. Dang, we're too late! It looks like they
> took Jack's wagon, caught it on fire, and then
> rammed it up to the cabin! Nate must have still

been alive inside, ran out, only to be butchered
by about twenty-eight gunshots. His friend Nick
Ray was shot in the back and died in the cabin.
His remains were burned up in the cabin fire.

Everyone present can see the note that has been pinned to Nate's
back: "Cattle thieves beware."

GEORGE. This is outrageous! Nate was no cattle
thief. He was one of the nicest men around!

WILLIAM. This has to stop. The cattle barons have
obviously hired some gunmen and are paying
them to hunt down independent cattlemen. We
can't let them get away with this murder spree!

SHERIFF. Look, I see Jack returning.

Jack gallops up, his horse worn-out from running fast. Jack jumps
off his mount.

JACK. Sheriff, the men are staying at the TA Ranch.
I believe they still have fifty men. The buildings
at the TA Ranch are well fortified, and it looks
like all the men have repeating rifles, much
better than our guns or ammunition.

Jack looks down.

JACK. Oh my God, is that Nate?

ALBERT. Take it easy, Jack. You did all you could.
He was out numbered.

SHERIFF. Okay, let's head back to Buffalo and
get ourselves a posse. We'll see if the shop

owner will let us use his rifles and ammo. Once townspeople hear about this murder, I have a feeling we won't have to worry about getting a large number together.

They temporarily bury the bodies of Nate and Nick. They then head back to Buffalo. Albert, William, and George break off toward Trabing and the inn. They need their own supplies and need to tell their family members why they are so late and what they will be doing.

> GEORGE, *to Sallie*. You know I need to go. We can't have this constant fear that the cattle barons will send someone to simply murder us in our sleep. They have no rights to restrict us branding mavericks and having our own brands and cattle. And then they keep us from sending them to market!

> SALLIE. I know, I'm just afraid for you…and for me and the children. What would I do without you?

> JESSIE, *to William*. Same here. I love you so much, William. But I know as a man you need to do what you feel is right. Would you wear this amulet around your neck? It will bring you good luck.

> WILLIAM. Sure, I will.

He takes the metal object and places it around his neck under his shirt.

> ALBERT, to Lucy. Jack was so scared. He and Alonzo almost died today. It would have devastated my sister. I'm going to join Jack and bring these murderers to justice!

LUCY. Well, I think I know how Imogene would
feel, because I feel that way right now.

A tear comes to her eyes, and Albert wipes it gently away. They all give their mates a good hug and then leave with their supplies and rifles, placing them on their horses. They then ride away to meet up with the rest of the posse at the TA Ranch.

Chapter 19

Buffalo, Wyoming, April 10, 1892

When Sherriff Angus gets to Buffalo and the city is informed of Nate's murder, a riot almost breaks out. It becomes easy to get men to volunteer for their friend's revenge, and eventually two hundred men are enlisted to go to the TA Ranch. The shop owner Robert Foote opens his hardware store and freely gives out rifles, guns, and ammunition. They all head out to the TA Ranch to seek justice.

Robert Foote mounts his all-black stallion and rides throughout the streets.

> ROBERT. Come on, citizens of Buffalo. Come
> join this fight for justice! Take arms. Come to
> my store and I will loan you rifles and guns and
> ammunition to take back our county!

> ANGUS. I need men who will join me for a posse.
> We are headed for the TA Ranch to arrest the
> "regulators." We need to defend our homes from
> the mercenaries that have been hired by the
> cattle barons!

Robert opens his hardware shop, and there is a rush by the volunteers to obtain guns and ammunition. There is even dynamite.

The womenfolk join in by having a potluck so that the volunteers have plenty of food and drink before they leave. They also prepare food to go.

> ROBERT. Take what you need. Come in and
> help yourself. Here are blankets and clothes.
> Whatever is needed to defeat this evil.

As the men gather together in the streets on horseback, Angus organizes them.

> ANGUS. All right, men, now is the time to ride out
> to the TA Ranch. I want fifty men under Jack
> Flagg. I want another fifty men under Arapahoe
> "Rap" Brown. Another fifty men under Robert
> Foote. And the remainder will be under myself.
> We will surround the TA Ranch and force them
> to surrender. Let's go!

All the men start out. As they get closer to the TA Ranch, other horsemen join them, such as Albert, William, and George. George rides up to Angus.

> GEORGE. Howdy, Angus! We're ready to join you.

> ANGUS. Glad to see you. The three of you can join
> Rap. See you at the ranch!

George pulls his horse away from Angus, then rides up to Albert and William.

> GEORGE. We've been assigned to Rap. Let's join
> his group.

They all start over to the group that is being led by Rap.

> GEORGE. Hi, Rap! Angus has assigned us to you.

RAP. Get with the rest of my group behind me. We
will be headed to the west of the ranch.

The three join the other fifty men.

TA Ranch, April 11, 1892

The TA Ranch is surrounded by the posse. Although outnumbered,
the "regulators" have an advantage with modern rifles and fortified walls.

ANGUS. Dang, our rifles are just not powerful
enough to get close to the regulators!

JACK FLAGG. We need to do what they did to
Nate. We need a breastwork so that we can get
up close and use our dynamite!

RAP. I agree. I'll get our men working on a
breastwork using bunkhouse logs perched on a
wagon frame. I'll let you know when it's ready.
I even have a name for it. We will call it the Ark
of Safety.

ANGUS. Okay. Do it quickly.

GEORGE. Hey, Angus, look at that guy shooting
from that hill over there. He has some type of
old muzzleloader. It really packs a punch. It just
took the hinge off that front door! I wish we
all had a powerful gun like that one. This fight
would be over.

ANGUS. Well, we have another plan. Hey, look,
there is a man on a horse coming out of the
barn. He's waving a white flag! Why, it's Mike
Shonsey!

MIKE. Don't shoot! I have a white flag. I want to
parley.

ANGUS. Okay, come out and let's talk.

But as Mike comes out, he suddenly spurs his horse and rides quickly past the surprised defenders. Although some shots are fired, he is able to escape.

ANGUS. Well, that is a disturbing turn of events.
Who knows where or what he will do? Come
on, let's get that breastwork started!

Mike knows that the telegraph wires are dead, because he helped to cut them. But he also knows that if he rides one hundred miles to the south, to the town of Gillette, he will have open wires. He heads there.

April 12, 1892

The defenders are continuing to work on the breastwork, but Rap has come up with another idea.

RAP. Angus, I have another idea. We should get a
cannon. If we had a cannon, then we could end
this siege.

ANGUS. Where do you think we could get a
cannon?

RAP. From Fort McKinney. Robert Foote has one of
the best horses around, so we ought to send him
to get a cannon.

ANGUS. Well, it's worth a try. Go tell Robert your
plan.

Rap rides over to Robert.

> RAP. Robert, I just talked with Angus, and he
> thinks we should go get a cannon from Fort
> McKinney. You have the best horse around. Are
> you willing to go?

> ROBERT. Yes. Here I go!

He gallops quickly away and reaches Fort McKinney. As he rides
up, he is met by guards. When he tells them his story, they are a little
unbelieving. Fifty hired guns being besieged by two hundred civilians.
He is taken to the commander of the fort.

> COLONEL JAMES JUDSON VAN HORN
> COMMANDER. So, you want a cannon to shoot
> other men out of fortified buildings.

> ROBERT. Yes.

> VAN HORN. I'm sorry, but this just sounds too
> bizarre. Plus, allowing you to shoot other
> civilians, who have not been convicted of a
> crime, is a crime in itself. I am denying your
> request.

Robert rides back to the TA Ranch.

> ROBER, to Rap. I'm sorry, Rap, but the
> commander at Fort McKinney has denied your
> request for a cannon.

> RAP. Dang, we could have ended this now.
> Hmmmm, I have done some blacksmithing.
> I think I can build my own cannon. I'll start
> working on it.

It takes most of the day for Rap to complete his project, but he actually makes a small cannon.

> ANGUS. My gosh, Rap, you really did it! You built
> your own cannon.

> RAP. I got the fuse in it, so here it goes.

He lights the fuse, and there is an explosion. The only problem is, while the cannon has exploded apart, it has done no damage to the fortified buildings.

> ANGUS. Well, we still have the Ark of Safety. It is
> almost done.

> RAP. It better work. We are out of options and
> getting low on ammunition.

Gillette, Wyoming, April 12, 1892

Meanwhile, Shonsey has reached the telegraph wires in Gillette, Wyoming. He sends a message to the acting Wyoming Governor, Dr. Amos Barber, who sends a message to President Benjamin Harrison. He, in turn, sends a message to the US Secretary of War, Stephen B. Elkins. Elkins then calls upon the Sixth Cavalry at Fort McKinney, led by Colonel James Judson Van Horn, to proceed to the TA Ranch.

Shonsey brings his horse into Gillette, Wyoming, and stops in front of the telegraph office. He quickly dismounts and runs in.

> SHONSEY, *to telegraph operator*. Are your lines
> working?

> OPERATOR. Why, yes, they are.

> SHONSEY. Good. I need to send a telegraph
> to the acting Governor Dr. Amos Barber. It

needs to say, 'Governor, I represent members
of the Wyoming Stock Growers Association.
We were trying to arrest cattle rustlers when
we were surrounded at the TA Ranch near Fort
McKinney. We need your help as we believe this
civilian organization will not let us surrender
or obtain justice. Please send troops as soon as
possible. Send that right away.

OPERATOR. That will be fifty-six cents.

Shonsey places his hand in his pocket and pulls out some change
and throws it on the counter.

SHONSEY. Keep the change.

The operator sends it right away. On the other end, an aide to the
Governor receives the telegraph and runs to the Governor's office. He
knocks on the door.

ACTING GOVERNOR DR. AMOS BARBER. Yes,
come in.

The aide opens the door quickly and runs up to the Governor.

AIDE. This just came in. It needs immediate action.

Dr. Barber takes the paper, reads it quickly, and picks up the phone.

DR. BARBER. Operator, I need to make a long-
distance phone call to President Benjamin
Harrison, Washington, DC.

There is a pause as the connection is made.

DR. BARBER. Mr. President, this is acting Governor Dr. Amos Barber of the great state of Wyoming. I have an emergency. There is a major conflict occurring on the TA Ranch near Fort McKinney, in which fifty men who are trying to control rustlers in our state have been surrounded by two hundred civilians. Our state forces are unable to control this situation, which could result in many civilian deaths. We are requesting that the President request that Fort McKinney send in troops from the Sixth Cavalry.

PRESIDENT. This is quite unusual.

DR. BARBER. Yes, Mr. President, I know this is unusual. I cite Article IV, Section 4, and Clause 2 of the US Constitution, which gives you authority to send in troops for domestic disputes.

PRESIDENT. Well, it sounds like you have assessed the situation carefully and you are aware of the need for our support to stop this action I will send out troops.

DR. BARBER. Thank you, sir.

Meanwhile, at the White House…

PRESIDENT BENJAMIN HARRISON, *hanging up the phone.* Well, that certainly sounded important to the Governor. They are a new state, and it certainly would show federal cooperation if I authorized our troops to help out.

He gets on the phone.

> PRESIDENT. Operator, get me US Secretary of
> War, Stephen B. Elkins.

There is a large pause.

> PRESIDENT. He's not answering in his office?
> Then get me at his home, right away. Hello,
> Elkins, this is the President. I need your
> cooperation right away. I need you to contact
> Fort McKinney and send out the Sixth Cavalry
> to the TA Ranch near Buffalo, Wyoming.
> We need this right away. There is a domestic
> disturbance involving fifty men arresting
> rustlers and two hundred civilians.

> ELKINS. Yes, Mr. President, I can contact Fort
> McKinney and get those troops out right away.

> PRESIDENT. Thank you.

At this point, Mr. Elkins is attempting to contact Fort McKinney, but there is a delay because the telegraph wires have been cut. However, he has been assured that a repair crew is already working on the situation and will have the lines connected by midnight.

Elkins approaches the telegraph office to wire Fort McKinney, which does not have a phone connection.

> ELKINS, *to operator*. I need to send a message to
> Fort McKinney.

> OPERATOR, *attempting to make contact*. I'm sorry,
> sir, there seems to be a problem with the lines.
> Let me try to assess the situation.

The operator leaves the room and comes back with some information.

> OPERATOR. Apparently, someone cut the
> telegraph wires near that area and we are unable
> to connect with Fort McKinney. However,
> I have been assured that a repair crew is on
> the way and that we will have service around
> midnight tonight.

At midnight, Elkins returns.

> ELKINS. Is the line open to Fort McKinney?

> OPERATOR. Yes, I am getting a signal back. Do
> you wish to send a message?

> ELKINS. Yes. To Colonel James Judson Van Horn,
> Fort McKinney, Wyoming. "Send out the
> Sixth Cavalry immediately to the TA Ranch,
> eleven miles from your fort. Assess situation
> between fifty men trying to apprehend rustlers
> and a two-hundred-civilian posse. Take actions
> as necessary to restore peace. Wire back to
> summarize outcome."

The telegraph wire goes out to Fort McKinney.

> TELEGRAPH OPERATOR IN FOR McKINNEY.
> Boy, look at this, a wire from the US Secretary of
> War. Take-over, Hugo. I have to get this to Colonel
> Van Horn right away.

Hugo gets up and takes over the operator's chair as the operator runs out the door to the officers' quarters. It is about 3:00 a.m. He knocks on the door to Colonel Van Horn's room.

COLONEL VAN HORN. What... boy, this better
    be good. Who is it?

OPERATOR. I have an important telegraph, sir. It
    is from the US Secretary of War.

COLONEL. That's good enough. Come in.

The operator quickly opens the door and rushes in, handing the
paper to the Colonel.

COLONEL. Thank you. You can leave. (*To himself,
    but out load.*) What the hell! There will be no
    sleep tonight.

He gets his uniform on and walks out of the barracks to the bugler.
He grabs him and pulls him out with his horn into the parade grounds.
The bugler lifts the horn to sound the alert. Lights start to come on
inside the enlisted men's barracks. You can hear men starting to get up
and get dressed. Some swearing is just audible through the walls. They
start to rush out of the doorways and line up in front of the Colonel.

COLONEL. Men, we have been ordered by the
    President of the United States through the
    Secretary of War to ride into the TA Ranch to
    assess needs to quell a domestic situation. There
    are fifty men surrounded in the ranch, with
    two hundred or more civilians surrounding
    them. It is believed that the fifty men that have
    been surrounded were trying to submit rustler
    warrants to some of the men that have them
    surrounded. These are White men, not Indians,
    and so we need to try to resolve this issue
    without bodily harm to any of the participants.

PRIVATE. Sir, do you think this has anything to do
     with Robert Foote earlier this day? He wanted a
     cannon from our fort.

COLONEL. Yes, I believe it is related. Now let's get
     our supplies, ammunition, and horses. We leave
     in thirty minutes. I want to get there as the sun
     starts to rise.

The men leave to get their supplies, rifles, ammunition, and to get
the horses ready for the march to the TA Ranch. As they line up by twos,
the Colonel looks over the troops and then waves his hand forward to
start their movement. The gates to the fort open, and they leave.

TA Ranch, Wyoming, April 13, 1892

As the sun is rising, the cavalry finally reaches the top of a hill. They
could see the conflict below in the valley. Crazy Woman Creek meanders
several times below. As described, hundreds of men are involved, and
activity has already started. They are approaching from the north to the
south. They can see a large movable breastwork being pushed from the
west to the east, toward a fortlike building.

RAP. Come on, men! We need to push with all our
     hearts. We will get up near the fort structure
     and throw in the dynamite.

William and George are part of the forty men trying to get this
heavy wooden structure closer to the regulators. Just then, a bullet gets
through one of the gun holes and hits William in the chest. He falls
back, and George rushes to his side.

GEORGE. William! You okay? William, get up!
     Come on, man, we're almost there. Don't

you die on me! Oh my God, no! This can't be happening to you.

He raises William's limp body up toward him, shaking him, pleading with him to wake up. Suddenly, there is some movement.

WILLIAM, *groaning*. Mmmm.

GEORGE. Where are you hit? William, answer me.

William searches his chest and pulls up his amulet from Jessie. The metal object now has a bullet lodged in it.

WILLIAM. Here…

He holds up the amulet, and it twists in the breeze. He smiles, and George gives out a sigh of relief.

GEORGE. Man, I thought you were a goner. You
    are so lucky!

They both get off the ground, and George gives William a hug.

WILLIAM. Ouch. That is going to be some bruise!

He rubs his chest. They both get up to the breastwork and continue pushing it forward.

RAP. We're almost there. I get the feeling that some
    of the men are going to realize that we have
    dynamite, and they will flee the fort. Then the
    other men can get them. Otherwise, they will be
    mincemeat.

Suddenly, there is a bugle call and the Sixth Cavalry comes down the hillside toward the breastwork. It stops moving, and Rap comes out to take a look.

> RAP. Damn it. Here comes the Cavalry. We were so
> close!

The shooting has stopped. The Colonel and his men set up a formation far enough away from the regulators that they will not be hit.

> COLONEL. What is going on here?

> SHERIFF ANGUS. Colonel, this posse has
> surrounded men who murdered Nate
> Champion and his partner, Nick Ray. There are
> about fifty men in these buildings, and although
> they say they have warrants for the arrest of
> rustlers, we believe that they have none and that
> they have a death list for innocent civilians.

> COLONEL, *to the men in the buildings*. You have
> heard what the Sheriff has to say. How do you
> answer?

A man comes out with a white flag from the "fort" building. It is Frank Wolcott, leader of the Wyoming Stock Growers Association.

> FRANK. Colonel, there are a lot of aspects to this
> situation that need clarification. I believe the
> best answer to quelling this conflict is for us to
> surrender and to give testimony as to what has
> happened here. I believe that once you have
> heard our side, we will be released.

SHERIFF. Colonel, you need to release these men
to me. They need a swift trial to determine their
guilt or innocence.

COLONEL. I believe that the citizens of Johnson
County would have a hard time giving these
men a fair trial. I am therefore going to take the
fifty men into custody, and I will take them to
Cheyenne, Wyoming. We will take testimony
here and at Cheyenne, then prepare a trial, if
necessary.

SHERIFF. Well, I have two dead bodies at the KC
Ranch to show that all fifty of these men need
to be tried for murder.

FRANK. Colonel, we will only surrender if we are
placed into your custody and not that of the
Sheriff.

COLONEL. So be it. All of you hiding in the
buildings, come out, and we will take you into
custody and send you to Cheyenne, pending a
trial if necessary.

Men start coming out from all areas of the buildings. They walk
up to Colonel Van Horn, their names are taken down, and eventually,
they are led away from the TA Ranch.

RAP, *to the Sheriff.* I can't believe this is happening.
We almost had them. We almost had justice for
the men they have slaughtered. Why did you let
the Colonel take them? By his taking them to
Cheyenne, I doubt if there will even be a trial.

SHERIFF, *to all the men.* Men, I know this is a
hard ending, but at least the barons know that
they cannot simply hire men to kill us. The
regulators that were here today will not return.
We will not let them return.

GEORGE, *coming out of one of the empty buildings.*
Sheriff, you need to see this. Looks like some of
the regulators shot themselves and died…

There is a rush by some to take a look.

RAP. By golly, they certainly did kill themselves just
crawling around like rats. Served them right!

Chapter 20

George Harris's Ranch, Trabing, Wyoming, 1893

The men are all sitting in the kitchen, discussing their options to survive the Johnson County cattle war.

> WILLIAM. We received no justice. The gunmen were released from jail, and they have all fled back to Texas.

> GEORGE. I know. There will be no change here, the water supply, the barbed wire, the harassment. Perhaps it is time for us to go. I feel that the small rancher has to always check their back.

> ALBERT. We have our families to watch out for.

Minihie and Josie have entered the home. They report they had a visitor from the Tongue River Reservation for the Northern Cheyenne. Minihie has not been feeling well.

> MINIHIE. We need to call the girls in for this conversation.

William gets up and goes to get them. They all cluster together while Minihie talks.

> MINIHIE. We had Black Wolf and old Little Wolf come to our home the other day. Josie and I have talked this carefully over. We come to you knowing that this would make a big change in our lives, but a necessary one for our safety and that of the children. I have seen the dangers increase over the last five years. I feel, as Josie does, that if we do not take up this offer, many will be killed. As you know, when the Northern Cheyenne were moved to the Oklahoma Territory Reservation, they fled due to terrible conditions. Many of our tribe died from disease. There was not enough food, and some starved. The other tribes felt like we were intruders using up their resources. Little Wolf and Dull Knife fled the reservation to go North, back up to our ancient hunting grounds. We have all heard of how they split up. Little Wolf found sanctuary and kindness after being arrested. But Dull Knife's people were going to be sent back to Oklahoma. Rather than that, they fled Fort Robinson. They were hunted down and shot like animals. However, because of their suffering and sacrifice, it was decided that the Tongue River Reservation would be established. In 1887, the Dawes Act went into effect.

Minihie is getting weak. She looks at her mom.

> MINIHIE. Mom, can you take over? I'm feeling a little bad.

Minihie is helped into a chair. Josie looks at her daughter with a worried look but gets up and stands to give the rest of their information.

> JOSIE. Each Indian must return to his tribe and
> be issued land. If there are not enough Indians
> to claim the land, then the excess land will be
> sold off to the White men. The land our tribe
> has sacrificed for will be lost. They gave us land,
> and then they take it away. Black Wolf has come
> to encourage us to leave Wyoming to settle
> into the Reservation in Montana. Each head of
> household will get 160 acres of farming land or
> 320 acres of grazing land. We need to look at
> our options. Tribal members would continue to
> receive rations from the government. This would
> include meat, flour, sugar, coffee, and once
> a year, shoes, blankets, and clothing for each
> member of our tribe.

> GEORGE, *looking at William.* This would be
> our chance to make a new life. But will the
> reservation allow us to come with our wives and
> family? We are not a member of the tribe.

> ALBERT. We have done so much work here. How
> can we give this all up?

> WILLIAM. I know, but think of it. You might get
> 320 acres of land. But how can we do that?

> JOSIE. This is the surprise we have been offered,
> and I think it is unique among our tribe. They
> are willing to "adopt" you, William and George,
> and Albert.

WILLIAM. So we would be Native American White?

JOSIE. Yeah, I guess that is one way to say it. In this way you will all be members of the Northern Cheyenne. We must make up our minds quickly, or the land will be gone forever.

GEORGE, *to Sallie.* What do you think, sweetie We have lived here a long time.

SALLIE. I will always go or stay as you decide, but now we have 160 acres and there we can have 320. We have so many children now, but there each one would be left with a larger portion then here. And you could ranch without the fear of being shot in the back.

WILLIAM, *to Jessie.* How about you, Jessie?

JESSIE. It would be nice to be with my family members. We worry here about being alone, not having enough help if things get tough. On the reservation I would be happy.

ALBERT, *to Lucy.* I remember when you first came back from school. You felt bad that you could not be a Cheyenne. This would allow you to return to your roots. But I'm afraid that I might not fit in. George and William have a great deal more experience.

LUCY. Yes. I would like to be with my family on the reservation. I would like to be free again to express my Indian side. Don't worry, my husband. I will help you learn our language and our customs. You will make a great White Indian brave!

She and Albert chuckle as she slips into his lap.

> JOSIE. It will mean a big change for the children. Luckily, they are used to my tepee and they have some idea of our language and customs. They will be quick to understand.

> GEORGE. Let's take a vote. All those in favor, raise your hands.

They all raise their hands.

> GEORGE. We need to sell the inn. We can take our animals with us.

> WILLIAM. We will need at least three wagons, one for each family, and four horses for each wagon. We need rides for each adult male. And we could use the chuck wagon for our food and supplies together.

> ALBERT. It might be cheaper to get more mules or donkeys for the wagons instead of horses.

> SALLIE. It is several months to get to the Tongue River Reservation. The women will be in charge of the chuck wagon and make all the meals.

> ALBERT. Thank God!

They all laugh.

> JOSIE. Minihie and I will watch over the children.

MINIHIE. I'm a little tired. I'm headed back to the
tepee. See you all later.

She gives a small cough. It goes unnoticed by most, but Josie is
worried.

There is an excitement in the air, the same excitement that William's
parents must have felt when they left their old home for their new home.
There was a new hope that fear would change to happiness. There was
a hope that all would prosper.

Later that night, Josie comes to Jessie.

JOSIE. Will you come with me? I want you to see
your mom.

Jessie follows Josie into the tepee.

JESSIE. Mom, are you okay?

MINIHIE. Sure. I'm just tired. I guess so many
children now to watch over. It is a happy job,
don't get me wrong, it can wear you out.

JESSIE. Let me feel your head. She places her hand
on her forehead and pulls it back quickly with a
worried look on her face.

JESSIE. Oh my gosh, Mom, you're burning up!
Why haven't you told us how sick you are?

MINIHIE. I am usually the healer. But nothing
I have used has helped. I did not want to
worry you.

JOSIE. Daughter, I will fix up a sweat lodge and
    perhaps that will help. No protesting now. I am
    going to make one.

MINIHIE. Okay.

Josie and Jessie leave the tepee together.

JOSIE'S. Granddaughter, I am worried for my
    daughter. She has never looked so sick. Can
    you have your men help build the sweat lodge
    tonight? I could build it tomorrow, but I think
    she needs it right away.

JESSIE. Sure, Grandma, I will wake them and they
    can come out to fix one up.

Jessie goes back into the house, gets Sallie and Lucy.

JESSIE. Mom is running a fever. She needs a sweat
    lodge but I don't think we can wait for grandma
    to make one. We need to get our menfolk up
    and have them build it tonight so she can use it
    right away.

SALLIE. We'll get them up right away.

They all go their different directions to get their men.
    George, William, and Albert get up immediately. With directions
from Josie, they set up the lodge. The next morning, Minihie is much
worse. Her fever is higher, and she trembles and sweats more. Her cough
is deeper in her chest, and her nose runs.

SALLIE. Come on, Mom. The lodge is all ready.
    The men helped make it late last night, as soon
    as we told them you were sick.

Minihie enters with Jessie's help. She is weak and needs help to sit down. There are large rocks in the center already heated by a fire. As she sits near them, Jessie pours some water on them and there is a great quantity of steam. Minihie sits and sweats more as the steam starts to heat her up. Jessie, too, is there to make sure her mom is okay. When the lodge ceremony is done, Minihie is placed in the house and laid on a couch. They try to help her with soup.

> MINIHIE. Thank you, but I am not hungry. I do
> not think the soup will stay down.

> LUCY. Here is some water, Grandma. You need to
> drink it or you will become dehydrated.

> MINIHIE. Okay, I will try.

She takes the glass and tries to drink some. She is not able to drink much.

> JESSIE. More, Mom. You need to drink more!

But Minihie shoves the glass away and moves her back to everyone. The women all secure a blanket around her body and shoulders.

> JESSIE, *to William*. I am worried about this,
> William. In all my years, I have never seen her
> so sick. I'm scared.

> WILLIAM. She is getting the best loving care. She
> is surrounded by family.

> SALLIE. I am glad we are close by.

The next day, Jessie wakes up and prepares a small breakfast for Minihie. She places the items on a tray and takes the tray into the parlor, laying it down on the table near the couch. Her mom looked so peaceful she almost didn't want to wake her.

JESSIE. Hello, Mom, time to wake up.

Seeing no response, she placed a hand on her shoulder to wake her up; still no response. Now she is concerned. She goes to turn her body to face her, but it is rigid. The horror of the moment is seeping into her. Jessie recoils in sorrow.

JESSIE. Mom, wake up. Wake up, Mom! Oh my,
  Mom, you are gone so quickly. It cannot be!

She starts to sing the death song. Soon Sally, then Lucy, then all the menfolk come in. Some of the children have come down.

SALLIE. We need to get Grandma! I will go.

Sallie rushes out to get Josie and some of the children who were with her. George bends over to examine Minihie.

GEORGE. I'm sorry, she is gone. She has been gone
  for a while, probably soon after we placed her
  on this couch, or the early morning hours. She
  is gone. She is dead.

Josie comes in and joins in the death song with Jessie and Sallie. Lucy never learned it, but cries in the melody.

WILLIAM, *to Albert*. Help me clear the table, we
  can lay her body there for preparations.

ALBERT. Okay.

GEORGE. I can help too.

The kitchen table was cleared off, and the men lifted her body and laid it onto the table. The women will prepare her body for the funeral. Her finest outfit is placed on her after washing. She is wrapped in a blanket and will be placed on a funeral platform, high in a tree. The men find the tree and construct the platform.

> ALBERT. I know just the tree. It is further back
> into the wooded area.

> GEORGE. Yes, I know where you are talking about.

> WILLIAM. I will get the wood, nails, and hammer,
> along with the ladder.

They put the items into the wagon, and they ride the wagon up to the wooded area. They can see the tree, as it had been very big in its glory days but is now dead with no leaves.

> GEORGE. Is that the one you were thinking of
> Albert?

> ALBERT. Yes, it will be perfect.

> WILLIAM. Minihie was such a wonderful person
> once you got past her distrust of all White men.
> I'm really going to miss her.

> GEORGE. I think we all feel the same way. It will
> be a nice resting place for her body, and in the
> traditional Indian way.

After much effort, the platform is completed. They go back to the house to get the body.

> GEORGE. It is time, Sallie. The platform is
> complete.

SALLIE. We are ready. Please come and take her
body into the wagon, and we will follow.

JESSIE. We will gather the children into another
wagon.

GEORGE. Albert, will you get the wagon ready
and drive that one?

ALBERT. Yes, and I'll drive slowly so the children
don't get scared.

They all follow the wagon with Minihie's body. The women and the older children walk beside. When they reach the tree, the wagons stop.

SALLIE. That is a grand platform.

JOSIE. Thank you for providing her with such a
wonderful resting place. Her spirit will be able
to find Ma'heo'o.

Using ladders, they place the body in its final resting place. Adults and all her grandchildren say their goodbyes. Her life story was their life story. Minihie would never see the reservation.

Chapter 21

*The Move from Trabing, Wyoming,
to Tongue River Reservation, Montana, 1894*

It takes a while to make all the arrangements to move. George shares the proceeds from the sale of the inn with William and Albert. They finally have everything ready in the spring of 1894. Upon their arrival at the reservation a special ceremony will be held to adopt all three of the White men.

> WILLIAM. How long do you think it will take to
> get to Lame Deer?

> GEORGE. If we were just on horseback it wouldn't
> take so long. But with all the wagons and
> children, it will be much longer. With all these
> supplies and people, it will take about one and a
> half months, maybe two months.

> WILLIAM. Then we need to go soon. This would
> be the best time to cross the rivers.

> ALBERT. Do we need to beware of any dangers
> along the trail?

WILLIAM. I'm afraid we will. We have been pretty
    isolated with our women and children, but
    the outside world has many prejudices about
    Indians. I think you saw that in Trabing, Albert.

ALBERT. Yeah. Indians are not allowed in
    many establishments. They are not served in
    restaurants or hotels. They are physically abused
    and often placed into jail, as if it is their fault for
    being Indian.

GEORGE. We all have to be watchful to protect
    our families.

It is time to go. Cattle and sheep are started with the dogs to help.
The best dog is Dune, a mutt, but mostly border collie. He has a good
ability to keep the herds together. He is the color of light beige sand
with long hair. Cleo is his mate. She is Black and White with long hair.
They would be invaluable in protecting the family at night. There are
four wagons, one for each family, and then the chuck wagon with all
the food supplies. They have all been on trips before to hunt for orphan
calves, but this is going to be a challenge. They skirt Trabing and head
for Sheridan, Wyoming. Before that, they have to cross a major river.

WILLIAM. Boy, that looks pretty deep and wide.
    I'm concerned for the wagons and our family.

JESSIE. I'm scared, William. I never learned how to
    swim. All I can remember is almost drowning in
    Sand Creek.

GEORGE. Don't worry, Jessie. We will send one
    man across with a rope, and we will string it
    across the two banks. That way, we can all cross
    the river in the same spot. If a wagon turns over,

the occupants can grab the rope and walk or
swim across.

Jessie rubs her neck and remembers the horrors she witnessed. William
sees the look on Jessie's face.

> WILLIAM. If needed, I will jump in and save you.
> Don't worry.

> ALBERT. Let me cross with the rope. Then I will
> come back and help with crossing the wagons.

He takes a long length of rope and ties it on a very strong tree near
the bank. After tying the knot, he pulls on it to be sure it is tight. He
gets back on his horse, with the rope, and they walk into the water.
His horse is not too happy and gives some snorting and bucking type
motions, but Albert keeps control. When he gets on the other side, he
finds another tree, pulls the rope tight from the other side, and ties
another knot. Then he heads back. On his way back, his horse stumbles
on a rock. As it falls forward headfirst Albert is thrown forward into
the water. The horse continues walking toward the shore without him.
William grabs the horse's reins.

> LUCY. Oh my God, Albert!

Albert pops up, grabs the rope, and walks back to the shore.

> ALBERT. There you go, I thought I would
> demonstrate for everyone what it is like to grab
> the rope and walk to safety.

Everyone laughs as Albert tries to get most of the water out of his
clothes. Lucy is not as happy; she has their youngest child in her arms.

LUCY. Albert, you scared me! When we get to the
    other side, I am going to make you change into
    some dry clothes.

ALBERT. Well, I hope I am the only one.

He looks up at her, and she looks down at him. The look on their
face shows that they both know the true dangers of this journey and
that they love each other.

LUCY. Me too!

The wagons start across. George starts out first, slapping the reins
against the horses. They go slowly. The wagons bounce and lurch over
the rocks. Then William and Jessie follow. Jessie keeps a close eye on
where the rope is.

JESSIE. Okay, kids, if anything happens, I want
    you to grab the rope.

Sallie is the driver for the chuck wagon. She is the last to start across.
The donkeys are stubborn due to the sound of the rocks on their hooves.
They start to get skittery and refuse to continue. George comes back
over on horseback and grabs their harness. He starts pulling and yelling.

GEORGE. Come on, you stubborn asses, get going!
    Keep hitting them with the reins, Sallie!

Eventually, the donkeys start walking again, and they get across
heading up the bank.

SALLIE. That was scary! I wonder what it will be
    like at the next river crossing.

GEORGE. Yeah, I wouldn't want to lose all that
    good food.

SALLIE. Why, you rascal, is that all you're worried
about, just the food?

GEORGE. Of course not, sweetheart. The food's no
good without the best cook in the world.

Three Weeks Later, Sheridan, Wyoming

It feels like they have been on the road for a month, but it is only
three weeks. The children are cranky, and all the adults are exhausted.
They need more supplies, so the menfolk decide to go into Sheridan.
The wagons are placed near a creek, in the shade, and the animals are
placed in a meadow nearby. The women wanted to stay behind with the
wagons and all the children.

ED, *to his mom, Jessie*. I'm so glad we can run
around. My legs are cramped from sitting in the
wagon so much!

SALLIE, *to Jessie*. A bath in the creek will feel so
good.

JESSIE. We need to get the men in there right away.
I can hardly stand their aroma. Yuck!

LUCY. My butt hurts! It's hard riding on the wagon
seat. Every little bump goes right in my hips!

The children are all milling around. Some are trying to climb trees.
Some are resting, lying on the grass, until another sibling or cousin
dumps some dirt on them. The older keep an eye on the younger ones
to be sure they don't get too close to the water or wander off.

JESSIE. Now, you little ones, no drowning allowed.
I want the older children to make sure the
younger ones don't wander off. The women

folk are all going to take a much-needed bath in the creek. Your dads will be back soon from Sheridan.

She takes off with Sallie and Lucy. Josie is staying with the wagons as she is sleeping. They find some bushes near the creek and shed their dirty clothes. They brought new ones with them to put on.

SALLIE. Isn't this so nice? And oh so *cold!* Brrrrrr.

She walks slowly into the creek.

LUCY. Boy, I never thought cold water could feel so welcome. I feel like the Rock of Ages with dust all over me.

SALLIE. You shouldn't complain, my daughter. Just remember which wagon is in the back of the caravan, me, me, and me. I have been seeing, hearing, breathing, and tasting dust for the last three weeks. Yuck!

JESSIE. Maybe you should go in last. From what you said, you will get the creek all dirty.

They all giggle and splash the water at one another. Soon they are all getting out of the water and are getting their undergarments on when they hear horseback riders. They can tell it is not their menfolk, as the horses are headed toward town, not from town. Fear starts to trickle down Sallie's spine.

SALLIE. Hush, gals. I hear riders. Get your clothes on real fast.

Four men on horseback see the wagons up ahead. They look rough, unshaven, dirty and are chewing tobacco.

FIRST MAN. Hey, look up ahead. There are some wagons. Wonder who belongs to them.

SECOND MAN. We ought to find out. Maybe it will be "worth" our trouble.

THIRD MAN. Nothing like some easy money.

FOURTH MAN, *the heaviest of them all.* Maybe they have food. I'm sure hungry.

FIRST MAN, harshly. You're always hungry.

They ride up quietly toward the wagons and see some children playing. Meanwhile, the women have gotten all their clothes on, their wet hair dripping down their backs.

FIRST MAN. Looks like a village of half-breeds. Hey, boy!

He's looking at Ed.

FIRST MAN. What are you doing here?

ED. We're all headed to Montana, to Lame Deer. We're going to live on the Tongue River Indian Reservation.

FIRST MAN. Where is your pa?

ED. He's in Sheridan, getting supplies.

FIRST MAN. Where is your ma?

Ed hesitates. He suddenly realizes the danger they might be in.

SECOND MAN. Didn't you hear, Jim? He asked
you a question.

ED. She's nearby.

The three women are nearby, but they aren't sure if they should
make themselves known or not. Sallie makes the bold move. She heads
on into the camp.

SALLIE. Can I help you?

THIRD MAN. My, ain't she a fine squaw! Are ALL
these children yours?

Jessie decides to head in, but Lucy is going to hide out. She might
be needed later.

JESSIE. Can we help you? This is my sister, and
some of these children are mine.

FIRST MAN, *Jim.* Wow, we hit the jackpot, boys,
another squaw!

FOURTH MAN. You got anything to eat?

SALLIE. Yes, we can fix you something to eat.

SECOND MAN. Well, some of us are hungry, but
not just for food.

The second man gets off his horse and starts over to Jessie. Jim pulls
his gun out.

JIM. I know you don't want any of these cute little
kids to get injured, so just do what we tell you
and you won't be hurt either.

The men haven't noticed, but most of the children have sneaked away. Only the older boys are left as decoys so the youngest and the girls could get away.

> SALLIE. We understand. We have a chuck wagon
> here. I can feed you all.

The third man gets off his horse and approaches Jessie. She cringes at his approach. He smells bad. He reaches over to touch her long black hair. The second man can tell she is repulsed by his friend.

> SECOND MAN. Maybe you would prefer me. I
> just took a bath. I'm nice and clean.

Jessie pulls away with a fake smile and walks over to Sallie.

> JESSIE. Here, Sallie, let me help you. There are so
> many guests.

They start to get some food ready in a skillet on the fire. The four men are starting to get pretty touchy and feely.

> SALLIE. Hey, we won't be able to cook you that
> great meal if you keep distracting us. I don't
> want to burn it. Here, we have some nice, hot
> coffee to start you out with.

She lifts the hot pot off the fire while Jessie lifts the hot skillet. When Sallie slings the hot coffee all over man number 4, Jessie hits man number 3 in the belly with the skillet. When he bends over in pain, she whacks him as hard as she can over the head. As Jim reaches for his gun, Josie (who has been watching everything transpire from a wagon) rises up with a large knife and slings it into his back. He groans and falls. Lucy has jumped out from the woods with a large stick and hits man number 2 over his head and neck. He is now unconscious. All four men are either badly hurt or dead. The women hug one another and then give a thumbs-up to Josie.

> SALLIE. We need to tie them up before they
> wake up.

Jessie bends down to check on Jim, who has the knife in his back.

> JESSIE. I don't think this one will wake up. He's
> dead.

Lucy grabs some rope from a wagon, and they all take turns tying a man up. They put a blanket over the dead man, Jim. They go over and comfort the boys that stayed behind and give the all-clear sign (the sound of a bird) for the rest of the children to come out of hiding. Now they are glad that they had completed a drill just like this one before they started the trip. They were hoping they would never have to use it.

> JESSIE, *to Ben and Ed.* You did perfectly. You
> protected your brothers and sisters. You stayed
> as decoys while the rest went into hiding.

> SALLIE. I'm so proud of you all.

Ed walks over to Josie

> ED. That was so awesome, Great-Grandma! You
> really know how to use a knife. Can you teach
> me how?

> JOSIE. Yes, you will have plenty of time to learn.

After about thirty minutes, the men start returning from Sheridan. They see the extra horses in the distance.

GEORGE, *to William and Albert.* There must be
     trouble up ahead. I see horses near the wagons.

WILLIAM. Goddamn it, we need to get there right
     away!

They all spur their horses to a gallop with guns drawn. When they
arrive, they see the four men on the ground.

WILLIAM. Gee whiz, what happened here?

Sallie, Josie, Lucy, and Jessie take turns telling the story as it unfolded.

GEORGE. Well, you gals are a force to be reckoned
     with. But what do we do? Do we take them to
     town to be arrested? One of them is dead. Will
     they bring charges against Josie?

WILLIAM. It was self-defense.

GEORGE. I know that, but it is an Indian against a
     White man, and we all know there is no justice
     for the Indian.

ALBERT. We need to just go without them.

SALLIE. Unfortunately, they know where we are
     headed. Ed told them.

JESSIE. I would say that the men are so
     embarrassed by the fact that Indian women
     spoiled their plans that they will not say
     anything.

SALLIE. If they did cause any problems, you men
     could say that it was you who protected your

property from them. No one would believe the
truth.

ALBERT. It's true. It is even hard for me to believe
that our womenfolk could fight and win against
four armed men.

And thus, it was, when the men woke up and realized that there were
now three men in camp and they had been defeated by Indian squaws,
they left with their dead partner, never to be heard from again. Their
embarrassment was so great that they headed back home and tried to
forget about their defeat.

The wagon train heads out over the hills. Alban Jr. was just born
before their trip and is colicky.

LUCY. Hush now, little one. Poor thing, your
stomach hurts.

She rocks him as she tries to nurse him, but the wagon roughly
knocks them around.

ALBERT. Poor little guy. I'm sorry, Lucy, but we
have to keep going. After what happened near
Sheridan, we need to get as far away as possible.

LUCY. I know. It's hard to believe that we now have
five little ones. I am so happy to be going to a
place where we will have our own land and our
own ranch.

The wagon in front is George's. His oldest son, William G, is up
front with him. George and Sallie have eleven children on this trip. Only
one, George Jr., died before their journey.

WILLIAM G. I wish George could have been here
with us. He was such a happy baby.

GEORGE. Me too. It was a big blow to all of
us, but more for your mom. A mother starts
loving her baby the minute they know they are
coming. We usually start after they are born. We
have had twelve children, and your mom has
had thirteen with Lucy. George is the only one
that has died, thank God. We have been very
lucky. It was an accident. No one's fault. We
didn't see the rattlesnake until it was too late.
Maybe if it had been a smaller snake or he had
been bigger, he would be with us today.

WILLIAM G. I remember. I didn't think the pain
and sorrow would ever go away.

GEORGE. I don't think it ever does. You just make
room for others in your life, but you don't really
forget.

Jessie and William are in the third wagon.

WILLIAM. Would you have ever believed all
those years ago when you were teaching me the
Cheyenne language that one day we would be
married, with nine children?

JESSIE. And a set of twins to boot! I saved those
two for the last.

WILLIAM. I'm glad we named one of the twins
Harriet, so I can call her Hattie. Our little
Hattie was so small. She was too early. It was
still so hard to say goodbye to her. I remember
my mom telling me about the first baby she

gave birth to in Iowa. She lost that one, and even after all those years, she still mourned.

JESSIE. I know, William. She was no bigger than your hand. Our first one, Mary Gertrude, was so plump and healthy. Mary was your sister's name?

WILLIAM. Yes.

JESSIE. Soon after Mary was Benjamin. He is growing up so fast.

WILLIAM. I was proud of little Edward, and Benjamin, for staying when those four men came by.

JESSIE. All the boys that stayed showed great strength.

In the last wagon, the chuck wagon are Sallie and Josie.

SALLIE. I miss my mom.

JOSIE. So, do I. I wish she could have headed home like I am now. Thank you, Sallie, for providing me with a safe place to live all these years.

SALLIE. It has been an honor. And you have helped with these children, oh so many now, George and I with our eleven, Jessie with her eight, and Lucy with her five.

JOSIE. I suspect if the pattern holds true, Lucy will have more than that when we get to Montana.

SALLIE. I'm going to miss Wyoming. It is all I have known. I enjoyed the inn and the stage stop. I liked our home and everyone around. We will all be separate on our own parcel of land. We are not even sure if the parcels will be together.

JOSIE. Don't worry about it. In the Indian world, we are all together spiritually and we come together for many tribal events.

SALLIE. Just as the White man has a prejudice against the Indian, I am afraid of the prejudice the Indian will have for our White husbands and for our half-breed children.

JOSIE. The half-breed world has been around with us in many forms. Before the White man, it was between a captive and their owner or between one tribe and another out of alliance, such as the Lakota Sioux and the Cheyenne.

SALLIE. I just hope the outcome will be a good one for them.

JOSIE. They have all been raised to have good self-esteem. They will survive.

Chapter 22

Tribal Headquarters, Tongue River Reservation
Lame Deer, Montana
One Month Later

After another month, they finally arrive at Lame Deer, Montana. William rides up ahead of the wagons to let the Chief know that they are arriving soon. As the wagons and animals pull up to the headquarters for the Tongue River Reservation, Chief Black Wolf comes out in full ceremonial dress. He walks up to the head wagon, which is driven by George and William G. Harris.

> CHIEF BLACK WOLF. We have been waiting and
> preparing for your families. Your story is our
> story. It is the merging of two worlds. You can
> leave your wagons here with your animals.

All the people in the wagons dismount. Each group has their children together with them.

> CHIEF BLACK WOLF. Have you all decided to
> choose grazing land?

All three men. Yes.

> CHIEF. Then you will each have 320 acres. After
> your adoption ceremony, we will enter the Tribal
> Headquarter Building and you will sign papers
> for your land.

The Chief goes over to a small area set aside for the adoption ceremony, which is to be held outside of the main building in a tepee. As the partners enter the tepee, they can see a small fire and several men are there. They are in full regalia, which includes feathered headdress, leather clothing that is intricately beaded, and handheld drums and pipes. The drums start to pound softly. The Chief and some of the other Indians, along with William, Albert, and George, bend down and sit around the fire. The women remain standing along with the Indians that are playing the instruments.

> CHIEF. Do all three of you agree to uphold the
> rules, regulations, and beliefs of the Northern
> Cheyenne Nation?

> ALL THREE. Yes.

> CHIEF. And do you agree to raise your children in
> the Cheyenne way?

> ALL THREE. Yes.

> CHIEF. We will now pass the pipe, and each of you
> will smoke from it. This will seal the adoption.

The pipe is passed around, and all smoke from the pipe. William looks over at Jessie and can see that all the women are excited by the ceremony.

> CHIEF. You are all now members of the Cheyenne
> Tribe. Follow me to the deeds.

The women walk up to their menfolk, pride beaming from their faces. They are all now members of the same tribe. They all walk through the entrance to a small building. As they enter, they can see an oak desk against a wall. Above it is a large map.

> CHIEF. Please sign the deeds. Per your request, I
> tried to situate your lands as close together as
> possible, but neither of these lands is next to
> each other. Those lands had already been taken.

Ration day is on the first Monday of the month. It is important that you take the ration cards up to the ration window and pick up your items. Articles of clothing, such as blankets, clothes, and shoes, are only given out once a year for each member of your family. It is important that you let the Bureau of Indian Affairs, or BIA, and the tribal offices know of any changes in your household, such as births, deaths, and marriages. You cannot drink alcoholic beverages on reservation land. This is strictly enforced by the tribal police. Once a year a census is held. It is vital that you are helpful and give them the information that they ask for. Currently, they are asking for your Indian name, the translation of your Indian name, the Christian name you have chosen, and your surname. It is important that you specify what you want as your last name or surname. Our tribes have never had this custom, but we are trying to cooperate with the White man's system. They need to have this information for the rations. Are there any questions?

No one has any questions at this point. They are all shown (on a large map of the reservation) where their particular plots are. They have all agreed to help one another build their cabins, barns, and corrals. George and Sallie will be first. Josie will live with Sallie and George. William and Jessie will be next, then Albert and Lucy. The wagons can also be used for living space.

GEORGE. Well, let's get started!

They all get into their wagons and start out to George's parcel of land. It is years, and a lot of hard work, before all the families are settled.

Reservation, Lame Deer, Montana
Soon after Arrival

Humpback Woman / Josie is very happy to be back in her homeland. She reminisces about her life history, landmarks that she remembers, and recalls life with her mother, Twin Woman. She gets to visit with her daughter Aurora (Snake Woman), Minihie's half-sister, whom she has not seen for many decades, and she is very joyous. She and others in the tribe are glad to see her. But she also feels that now that she is "home" and her granddaughter and great-grandchildren are home, her duty is done. She could finally relax. Sallie and George initially make her a part of their home. Josie has set up her tepee on their property, but she becomes less and less able to care for herself. She needs help. And then her health starts to deteriorate. Early into her return to the reservation, she moves her tepee closer to the ration building and begins to share her home with her daughter Aurora (Snake Woman).

> SALLIE, *to George.* George, I was visiting near the
> ration building and saw Grandma's tepee. I'm
> not sure what to do for Josie. My relatives that
> live nearby state that she hardly leaves her tepee.
> She is hardly eating any food or drink. I am
> afraid.

> GEORGE. Maybe she would be better with us or
> Jessie or Lucy?

> SALLIE. She is limping, like she cannot walk well,
> and I am afraid she does not know how to take
> care of her tepee anymore. I am afraid that she
> will start a fire in the tepee and that she will
> catch on fire. She needs help. Aurora is there,

but she also goes to visit her own family as well. She is not there twenty-four hours a day.

GEORGE. Josie wanted to live in the traditional way, and Aurora still lives in the traditional way. It is what they both wanted.

SALLIE. I know. I think I will go to Aurora and ask her to help. I haven't seen her for a while. Are you okay if I have both Josie and Aurora come back to live with us? We would have to provide them with food and water. We have so many in our family already.

GEORGE. It's okay. Go get her, if you can.

Sallie leaves to see Aurora the next day. She lives closer to the government ration station, where she could more easily get her food. Sallie gets off her horse and Aurora hears, so she gets up and lifts the flap to her tepee. Unlike most of the modern tepees, which are made of canvas, they still live in buffalo hide. It is so old that most of the pictures are too faint to even see, and some of the flap is now fringed with wear.

AURORA. Why, my dear niece Sallie, I am so glad to see you! Please come in and share my warmth. What brings you here today, other than my company?

SALLIE. Aurora, can we talk outside?

AURORA. Sure, we can. Let's take a short walk.

SALLIE. I am worried about Grandma Josie. She is getting older, and I'm sure you have noticed that she is less able to care for herself. She does not want to join us in our home but wants to remain in the old ways, with her tepee. We are able to provide her with food and anything else she needs. She now has a limp. I am also afraid that because of her issues, she cannot make a fire in a safe way and may injure herself. I am here to ask you if you would consider sharing a tepee with your mother at our home, on our property, away from the ration building? George and I would provide everything that you need in the way of shelter, food, water, clothing, etc. You would not need to depend on the ration station.

AURORA. My children are close here, to the ration station, Bessie Rising Fire, Minnie Clubfoot, Frank Pine, and Peter Big Left Hand. My grandchildren are nearby also. It would be a hard decision to make. I understand the need for Josie. I must talk with my children and then give you my decision tomorrow. Can you come back?

SALLIE. Yes, I can come back. It is so important. I don't know what to do.

Sallie hugs her aunt and gets back on her horse for home. She arrives back at the ranch.

GEORGE. Well, how did it go?

SALLIE. I don't think she is going to do it. She has another life. She has four children, all with many children, and they need her. As much as she loves her mother, she loves her children as well. It would be a hard decision for me if I were faced with it too.

The next day, Sallie arrives at Aurora's tepee. Aurora goes outside to talk with Sallie.

> AURORA. I'm sorry, Sallie, I am not able to move from my current location. My life right now is close to the reservation with my children. They need me to help with all the grandchildren, and I wish to fulfill that responsibility.

Sallie decides to talk with her grandmother Josie, so she goes into the tepee. Josie sees Sallie and is very happy to see her.

> JOSIE. I heard you came to this area yesterday, but I did not see you. I am glad that you have come in to visit with your grandma.

> SALLIE. Grandma, I care for you very much, but most of the time there is no one in your tepee to help you with your daily chores. I worry about you. I want you to be safe and healthy. I want you to come live with George and me in our home.

> JOSIE. No, I will not leave this tepee. All my life I have lived in this one or one like it. It is my way of life. To take me out would be to kill my way of life. It would kill me.

> SALLIE. But, Grandma, I have noticed that you limp. It is hard for you to get food and water, so you need to come into the home with us. I am not able to have anyone come live with you in your tepee, so George and I would love to have you move into our cabin.

> JOSIE. Who did you ask to come into my tepee?

Sallie realizes that she may have touched on a tough area. That her own daughter would not come to be with her.

SALLIE. I asked Aurora…

JOSIE. I see. Thank you, Sallie, for caring so much
for me. Let me think about this.

Sallie gets up and hugs her grandmother and leaves the tepee for the ranch.

GEORGE. Did Josie agree to come into the cabin?

SALLIE. I don't think so. I slipped up and told her
that I had asked someone to stay with her. I
had to tell her that I asked Aurora and that she
was not going to come. I could not tell, but I'm
pretty sure that it hurt Josie's feelings.

GEORGE. We can check on her tomorrow
morning and find out what her answer is.

SALLIE. Okay.

The next morning, Sallie gets up, makes some food, and decides to take some out to Grandma Josie. As she approaches the tepee, Josie is not there. Some of her personal items are missing, including her blanket, her ritual hide scraper, and a deerskin. Aurora comes running into the tepee.

SALLIE, *to Aurora*. Where is Grandma?

She can see the worried look on Aurora's face and suddenly realizes what may have happened. Josie has left for the "death walk!"

SALLIE. What have you done, Grandma? Where
have you gone?

AURORA. I have alerted my family. They are out
looking for her right now. She may have left last
night.

Sallie gets back onto her horse and gallops back to the ranch. She
gets off quickly and runs up the stairs and into the house.

SALLIE. George! George, come here quick!

George runs into the room.

SALLIE. I think Grandma has gone on a death
journey. She probably feels like her days are
numbered, that she is no longer helpful, and
that she is seeking death. I've done this to her.
(She sobs.)

George grabs Sallie by the arms.

GEORGE. Don't blame yourself. Your grandmother
has lived the old ways all her life. This is all part
of it. The elderly sometimes picks the time to
complete the cycle of life. You know this better
than most.

SALLIE. We need to go find her. I don't want her to
be doing this because she does not believe that
she is loved and cared for.

GEORGE. Yes, I will head out, and I will go get
Albert. He is close by. We will have twice the
luck in finding her. Don't worry, sweetie.

He hurries out of the room, gets dressed, heads out to the barn, and
gets his horse and an extra one for Josie. He then gallops to Albert's and

Lucy's farm. Albert can hear a horse coming and heads to the porch to see who it is.

> GEORGE. Albert, Josie has gone on a death
> journey. Sallie needs us to go bring her back.

> ALBERT. A death journey? Why would she go on
> one of those?

> GEORGE. It's a long story. I'll tell you on the way.
> Get your horse and come join me. She probably
> left last night, and it was really cold.

> LUCY. What's wrong, Albert? Did I hear you say
> Josie is on a death journey? Oh my God, you
> need to find her right away.

> ALBERT. We'll do the best we can.

He gets his boots and coat on and runs to the barn to get his horse.

> ALBERT. Come on, George, let's go.

They kick their steeds and head off in a gallop.

> LUCY. I must go to Mom. Come on, kids, we're
> headed to Grandma's!

She gets them all ready, hitches up the wagon, and they head off to Sallie's. As she approaches, Sallie comes out, crying.

> LUCY. Mom, don't cry. They are going to find Josie.

> SALLIE. I hope so. I feel so guilty. Come in out of
> the cold and get those kids into the warmth.

Several hours later, George and Albert return to George's cabin. A body is lying over George's spare horse. Their faces are cold and sad. Lucy and Sallie hear them coming and have rushed out to the porch to help Josie into the house. They are not expecting to see her body draped over a horse.

SALLIE. No! No! I did this…

She starts to fall to the ground, and Lucy catches her and helps her kneel on the porch. George dismounts and goes to Sallie.

GEORGE. It was Josie's choice. We must respect
her wishes. It is the old way, hard for us to
understand in this time and age, but part of her
upbringing. You have to forgive yourself.

The other members of George's family have come out also. The daughters help Sallie to her feet, and they take her in. Albert and George take Josie's body into the home. The daughters have already cleared the kitchen table to prepare the body. Like with her daughter Minihie, Josie is placed on a high scaffold. Her blanket, deerskin, and hide scraper are with her. Many of the old members of the tribe come to mourn, as do her daughter Aurora and her family. Sallie, Lucy, and Jessie and their families give speeches about their lives together and how Josie had saved Minihie, Jessie, and Sallie at the Sand Creek Massacre. Because most members of the tribe were descendants or relatives of Humpback Woman, her life and legacy really made a difference in the tribe.

Chapter 23

The Harris Family Cabin
Northern Cheyenne Reservation, 1901

SALLIE, *to eldest daughter, Julia.* Julia, where is
George?

JULIA. He went outside to cut some wood.

SALLIE. I told him not to do that. I told him
Albert would be coming tomorrow.

JULIA. But we are almost out of wood, and it is
very cold. We will not last until tomorrow.

SALLIE. I'll get my coat on. Lunch is ready.

She gets her shoes and coat on, with a shawl around her head, and
steps out. She walks around to the wood chopper in the back. She stops.
Something is not right. She should be hearing the sound of the wood
being chopped or movement of George laying up the log pieces. A small
amount of snow is falling, and she does not see any footprints. She walks
further around the house. And then she sees him lying on the ground,
covered with a small amount of snow.

SALLIE. Oh, George!

She screams. She runs to him and turns him over as he is facedown. He is still alive, but his breathing is shallow. She calls for her son.

SALLIE. William! William, come quickly!

GEORGE. Sallie, my heart, I think this is the end.
So painful…I love you, forever, I love you…

His breathing stops, his body goes limp, and Sallie starts to cry and scream. She tries to sing the death chant but can't. William G makes it over from the barn.

WILLIAM G. What is it, Mom? Dad! What
happened? Is he hurt?

SALLIE. Your father is dead. He said it was his
heart. Oh, William!

WILLIAM G. Mom, let me get you in the house.
There's nothing else you can do out here. I'll go
get James, Charles, Edward, and Henry. We will
help carry Dad's body into the house. Come on,
it is too cold out here.

SALLIE. Why didn't he ask you boys? Why didn't
he wait for Albert?

WILLIAM G. We are all helping with the stock. We
are feeding the cows and sheep. We have to take
the hay all over the range with the wagons. I'll
get the others. Let's get you into the house.

William G. helps Sallie up from her knees. Her grief is great as he walks her into the house.

SALLIE, *to Julia.* Your father is dead. He told me it
was his heart. He died in my arms.

As she opens her arms to show how she held him, she begins to sob uncontrollably. Julia grabs her and hugs her; Sallie's other daughter's run in, and they help their mom to a couch. Meanwhile, William G. has found his other brothers and told them of their father's death. They abandon their feed wagons and ride their horses in together. They go to the back of the house.

> HENRY. I can't believe he is dead. I always thought
> he would live forever.

> EDWARD. He was a great man and the leader of
> our household. He was wise and good to us.

> JAMES BRYAN, *to Charles.* Help me get him up.

Charles and James bend down, but even the two cannot pick him up, so four of the brothers pick him up and all of them, except William, go into the house. William picks up the ax and starts to strike the pieces of wood.

> WILLIAM G, *to himself.* I need to finish my dad's
> work. I will miss you, Dad. We'll take care of
> Mom for you. You raised us to be responsible
> and to take care of family. Thank you!

He hits the wood very hard, over and over. The physical work helps him express some of the anger and despair he feels. As the body of George goes through the house, Sallie and Julia and her other daughters, Elizabeth, Emma, Louise, Jessie, and Alice, look on. Alice is only eight years old. All sob as he passes. Sallie and Julia both start the death chant. The kitchen table is cleared off, and his body is laid on it. The women gather together around his body to prepare it for burial.

The boys all linger in the parlor, talking together.

> JAMES. We need to let the other family know.
> I sensed that William needs to be cutting

the wood. I'll head over to Lucy and Albert.
Charles, you ride over to William and Jessie.

CHARLES. Okay.

JAMES. The rest of you head back into the field to
feed the animals.

The rest of the boys head out, and Charles gets on his horse to ride
to Jessie. James walks around the house to tell William. He finds him
in a manic phase.

JAMES. William…William!

William finally stops murdering the wood.

JAMES. I'm headed out to Lucy's to tell her about
Dad. Charles is headed to tell William and
Jessie. Are you going to be okay?

WILLIAM G. I'm just so damn mad.

JAMES. Me too. Be careful, William. I don't want
two funerals. We depend on you now, more
than ever. Dad always shared with you how to
run the ranch.

WILLIAM G. The girls taking care of Dad?

JAMES. Yes.

WILLIAM G. I'll head into Lame Deer in an hour
or so. I'll arrange for the plot at Lame Deer
Cemetery. He would want a White man's funeral.
And I will complete an obituary and inform the
Tribal Headquarters and BIA of his death.

JAMES. When Charles gets back, we will get
    Edward and Henry from the fields and we will
    spread out to tell our neighbors and other family
    members.

WILLIAM G. That sounds great. Thanks for taking
    on some of this responsibility. I couldn't do it
    without you.

Charles makes it to William and Jessie's ranch. He pulls up to their cabin. Some of the older children are busy with farm chores. Edward sees Charles ride up.

EDWARD. What a surprise, Charles. What brings
    you here?

CHARLES. I have sad news. My father died, and
    I need to tell Jessie and William. They need to
    come to our cabin to help my mom. She is not
    taking this well.

Ed runs into the house. Benjamin overhears the conversation.

BENJAMIN. It's hard to believe. He was like
    another father to us. How did it happen?

CHARLES. He was chopping firewood and had a
    heart attack. He died in my mom's arms.

William and Jessie appear on the porch.

WILLIAM. Thank you, Charles, for coming all this
    way. Our family will head over to your ranch.
    Do you want to come in to warm up?

CHARLES. No, thank you. I need to head back.

He pulls the reins of his horse to move him in the correct position and spurs him onward.

> JESSIE, *to William*. Sallie must be so sad. I can't
> imagine her grief. She loved George so much,
> like I love you.

She looks up in William's face with tears running down her face. What she wasn't expecting are the tears she sees in William's eyes.

> WILLIAM. He was a good, good friend. I will miss
> him and his humor.

William checks his watch to see the time. He also looks at the small locket on the watch fob. He places it back in and gives Jessie a hug. They walk back into their home. They start to get ready to head toward Sallie's cabin.

The wagon pulls up to George's ranch. The whole Bixby family is there, William, Jessie, Benjamin, Edward, James, Mary Gertrude, Anna E., and the twins, Louisa and Harriet. Jessie runs into the house while the rest get out of the wagon. As she enters, she can hear the death chant being sung by Sallie and Julia. When Sallie hears Jessie's steps, she quickly turns and rushes into her arms.

> SALLIE. Oh, Jessie, he's gone to be with Ma'heo'o.
> I at least got to see him as he left this world. He
> was in so much pain.

She starts to sob on Jessie's shoulder.

> JESSIE. Here, sit down. We'll get through this
> together.

> JAMES, *to Sallie*. Hi, Mom. I just got back from
> Lucy's. She and the clan will be here soon. Oh,
> hi, Aunt Jessie.

JESSIE. Hi, James. Thanks for doing that. Where's
William G?

JAMES. He went to Lame Deer to make the
arrangements for the grave site and to let the
tribe know of his death.

By now George's body has been cleaned and new clothing placed
on him. William goes up to his body.

WILLIAM. Hey, old friend, what's the idea of
leaving me? I always thought I would go first.
You were a good role model. You taught me how
to love.

Flashback Memories

- Their first meeting on the train to Fort Laramie, and the building
of Fort Fetterman.
- William in the wagon with George as they are escaping from
Indians to Fort Fetterman.
- William going with George to meet Sallie's family.
- William as best man at George's wedding to Sallie.
- Helping George build his cabin/inn at Crazy Woman Creek.
- George as best man at his wedding to Jessie.
- George helping him after being shot at the TA Ranch.
- Their travel to the reservation and their adoption by the tribe.

George's daughters are sitting nearby. William's daughters come
up and start talking to their cousins. A wagon is heard pulling up. It is
Lucy and Albert and their children, Alfonso, Deyos, the twins (Kittie
Belle and Julia Agnes), Alban Jr., Roy Foy, Nellie Pearl, and James Pozy.
Lucy is pregnant with her next child, which they believe will be a boy,
Wolfert. James goes out to greet them.

JAMES. Welcome, sis. Jessie and Mom are in the
house.

Lucy looks at James. Her eyes are red, and she has a handkerchief in her hand.

LUCY. I can't believe that Papa is gone. He was one
of the greatest men I have ever known. I will
miss his strength and his love.

JAMES. We all will.

Lucy is helped down the wagon's passenger side. She walks quickly into the house. She sees her mom. Sallie is too weak to get up from the chair, so Lucy goes to her knees by the chair.

LUCY. Mama, I know your grief is great. What can
I do for you?

SALLIE. I will be going through much sorrow. Go
and see your dad. Say your goodbyes.

Lucy gets up and goes over. She grabs Albert to be with her. As she approaches, all her memories of her dad flow into her.

Flashback

- Lucy going up to George after he married her mom, calling him Papa.
- Lucy coming home from her schooling to reunite with her mom and dad.
- Lucy walking down the aisle with her dad at her arm as she marries Albert Spang.
- Their travels to the reservation.

She realizes that they will no longer share those memories. She starts to cry and sob. She finds comfort in Albert's chest. He directs her to a chair, and they both sit down.

> ALBERT. We both cared for your father. He gave
> me his respect and his trust. And he also gave
> you to me. Come on, sweetheart, calm down.

Flashback

- Albert being hired by George to cut wood for the inn.
- Albert sitting as a family member at a meal at the inn.
- Albert meeting Lucy.
- Albert marrying Lucy.
- Albert joining George for the Johnson County cattle war.
- Albert joining George to find Josie.

> LUCY. Mom says he was chopping wood and had a
> heart attack. He died in her arms.

She clenches her handkerchief and wipes tears away.

> ALBERT. I wish I had come a day sooner. He might
> still be alive.

He thumps his fist against his knee and gets up in anger with himself.

> LUCY. Dad was stubborn. He knew you were
> coming tomorrow. Don't blame yourself.

William walks around to all of George's daughters to give his condolences. At the end, he walks over to George's body again. He takes his watch out and looks into the locket. There is the painting of Oliver and Mary, so happy. This was the family that he left behind in Iowa and would probably never see again. Now, on the other side is a photo of him and Jessie. This is the family that he has now.

WILLIAM. George, old man, I'm glad I met
      you. Because you met Sallie, I met Jessie. And
      because Albert worked for us, he met Lucy. You
      were a kindhearted man. I have learned many
      life lessons from you.

Friends and relatives came by the wagonfuls. They all knew and admired George.

Sallie is helped through her sorrow. At the end of three days, George has a funeral at Lame Deer Cemetery. As members of his family stand near his casket, many of them have something to say to the whole group present that day.

SALLIE. Goodbye, my dear love. Thank you for
      being so good to me. I will miss you so much.
      Our children will take care of me now.

Flashback

- Sallie being rescued by George from Captain Cahill.
- George coming to Josie's tepee with gifts.
- Sallie giving birth and how George reacted to Lucy.
- George marrying her, and then their Indian wedding.
- George and Sallie at the inn and stagecoach station.
- Sallie and her worry about the Johnson County cattle war.
- Their journey to Lame Deer by wagon.
- George bringing Josie back after the death journey.
- His last words to her as he died in her arms.

She picks up soil and throws it onto his casket. Lucy is by her side to help her get back to her seat. William gets up and walks over to the casket.

WILLIAM. To our many years of friendship. I'm
glad we got to know each other, and I'm really
sorry to see you go.

He bends over.

WILLIAM, *in a whisper that no one else can hear.*
And while you're up there in heaven, will you set
up a space at that great poker table in the sky,
and I'll join you later?

He picks up some soil and throws it onto the casket.
Albert gets up and walks over to the casket.

ALBERT. You always treated me like family, and
then I became family when I married Lucy.
Thank you for helping me become the man I
am today.

He picks up some soil and throws it onto the casket.
The rest of the family members walk by and leaves their thoughts.
Many of the women have been crying. Their eyes are red, and they have
handkerchiefs in their hands. Some use soil, some use flowers and one,
his youngest daughter, leaves a small dream catcher. His coffin is lifted
up and down into the ground to lie beneath the Montana soil that he
had come to love.

Chapter 24

Sheridan, Wyoming, October 17, 1918

ED, *to his mom.* I remember Uncle George. He was
a great man, kind and gentle, but strong and
fearsome.

JESSIE. Like your dad.

She suddenly turns around and looks uphill.

JESSIE. We need to get back to the hospital to
check on your dad.

There is a new look of concern, as if she knows that something is
wrong. Ed takes his mom's arm, and they walk back uphill to the double
doors of the building that is now a temporary hospital. They arrive
at William's cot. He is coughing badly, and it looks like his fever has
returned. But worse yet, his face has turned a light blue.

JESSIE. William, can you hear me? Calm down.
You're going to tear your lungs out coughing
that bad. Is there any honey to help his cough?

MARY GERTRUDE. I have some left in the jar we
brought to help Dad while in the wagon. Here
it is.

Jessie takes it, her hands shaking, and unscrews the cap. She places
the spoon into the jar, takes a small amount, and places the honey into
his mouth.

JESSIE. William, this is some honey. Try to get
some into your throat. It should help you.

Eventually the spasms of coughing slow down and he has low
coughing. They can hear a rattling in his chest, like fluid is filling it up.
His daughters continue to attend to his needs by placing a cold compress
on his forehead to relieve the fever. Louisa and Harriett are identical
twins who like to dress alike.

LOUISA. Mama, Dad looks so bad. I thought he
was going to pull out of this, but he only got
worse.

HARRIETT. The doctor came by. He stated he
gave dad all the aspirin he could have, that
any more might kill him instead of the disease
he has.

MARY GERTRUDE. He's just got to get better.
Life just won't be the same without Dad.

BENJAMIN. Dad's parents both died together of
inflammation of the lungs. I bet it was the same
thing he has now.

JESSIE. Don't be too afraid of death. It is the
omega to the alpha of life. Poor Anna has had
to see two of her babies die, one just a few days

ago. I've lost three children, James, Maggie, and Hattie, the first one with that name. My mom died before we left for Montana, and my grandmother right after we arrived. Even Aunt Aurora died two years ago. If the worst comes to pass and my dear William dies, at least we know we did all we could and that his family was here to care for him. Death makes room for birth.

She pauses for a second, as if looking up at another day.

JESSIE. You remember our move from the reservation to Kirby? What a joyous occasion that was!

Kirby, Montana, 1914

Jessie and William are taking a walk around their ranch. There is plenty of water from the nearby stream. They have a ranch house and a barn. There is a corral with five horses. Some cattle can be seen in the distance. His sons and sons-in-law are hard at work tending to the harvest. They all have hats on to protect their necks and faces. Bandannas are around their neck to soak up the moisture.

WILLIAM. We finally made it, Jessie. We are still close to the reservation, but this is the bounty land I was able to receive due to my service, and what a paradise!

JESSIE. Yes, it is a blessing. Our children are growing, are getting married, and have children of their own. Most of them have stayed on the ranch, and we get to help one another. I am happy!

WILLIAM. I am glad that you and I both know
the Cheyenne language and can teach our
grandchildren. They would never get it in their
regular school system. I heard there is a Pow
Wow next week on the Reservation. We should
go and take the whole family.

JESSIE. I would love that. Our children and
grandchildren can benefit from both worlds. I
wonder what it will be like one hundred years
from now. Where will our children's descendants
be? What will they be doing with their lives?
Will they still be close to the reservation or far
away?

WILLIAM. We can only hope that they, too, will
have the love we have had, have children like
we have, are able to provide and protect them
as we have, and see the wonder of it all before
they die.

Ed comes running up to his parents with a Kodak Brownie camera
in his hands.

ED. Hey, I want to take your picture. I set up some
chairs nearby.

William and Jessie walk back toward the house and see the chairs.
They sit in them, and Ed takes their picture.

ED. Thanks, Mom and Dad. I feel that a picture is
like a time machine. Future generations will be
able to look at the two of you, and they will see
your life together as it is this very moment in
1914.

JESSIE. Well, if that is true, then I should have
    worn a different dress. This one makes me look
    like a balloon!

She chuckles along with her husband and son.

Sheridan, Wyoming, 1918

ED. Yeah, I remember taking that photo. We have it
    on the mantel of our fireplace.

The doctor, who looks like he finally got some rest, comes over to
look at William.

JESSIE. Doctor, why is William so blue?

DOCTOR. It is because of his lungs and his
    coughing. His lungs cannot transport enough
    oxygen to his vital organs, so they are taking the
    oxygen from the capillaries in his face. It turns
    his face blue. If you look around you can see that
    many patients have this symptom.

He listens to William's heart and to his pulse. He hears the fluids
filling up in his chest. His face saddens as he looks at Jessie.

DOCTOR. The disease has turned into pneumonia.
    Of the deaths from this disease, most of them
    die not from the disease but from the other
    problems that occur after they get it. Pneumonia
    is the one that kills the most. I don't have good
    news, Jessie. Love William while you have time
    with him. It won't be long. His lungs are almost
    full. There is nothing more I can do. I wish I
    could. Perhaps in the future doctors will discover

an agent that can fight back. But we have
nothing today. I'm so very sorry.

He looks away, almost in embarrassment; a family that he wants
to help, a man that he wants to save, but there is nothing he can do.
Eleven others have already died today. He can see in the far corner the
aides taking out the last victim through the back door to the mortuary.
He knows that William will be the twelfth.

Jessie has tears running down her eyes. The daughters start to sob.
Ben and Ed kneel down with their sisters. Ed grabs his father's hand.
Almost silently, under her breath, Jessie begins the death cry. The sun
has gone down, and the room, although with some artificial light, is
much darker than before.

> JESSIE. Thank you, William (sobbing), for
> providing me with love and affection. Thank
> you, William, for providing me with shelter,
> a home, and protection. Thank you, William,
> for so many wonderful children to carry on our
> love. They will now care for me as you cared
> for me.

William begins to gasp for air. His eyes look up toward Jessie with a
small tear. His hand grasps harder that of his son Ed. He takes his other
hand, reaches for his pocket watch, pulls it out, and hands it to Ed. His
body relaxes and air is breathed out. His eyes are open, but there is no
more movement. His life is over. The sobs are uncontrollable. Ben reaches
over and closes his father's eyes. The daughters are beside themselves,
but Jessie is stiff, unable to react. Ed sees what is happening to her; he
gets up, (holding the watch tight in his hand), goes over, and places his
arms around her shoulders. She starts to rock back and forth in despair,
and yet she knows this is a cycle that she has come to understand. But
this one is so much closer than all the others.

JESSIE, *in a whisper.* I will love you forever. May Ma'heo'o allow us to be together again.

The doctor can tell that something has happened and comes over again.

ED. It is done, Doctor. Our father is dead. We know you did all that you could. Whatever this disease is, there are many more suffering as he did. Have they given this a name?

DOCTOR. Yes, the Spanish Flu.

ED. We will not be leaving the body here. We will be taking our dad's body back to Kirby, Montana. We will need the death certificate. Can you mail this to us?

DOCTOR. Yes, I can do this for you. You have a family plot in Kirby?

ED. Yes, we have a family plot. We just buried one of my young nephews last week. He probably died of the same disease, but we had no name for it at that time. We have a wagon and will place my dad's body there. Do we need to do anything else?

DOCTOR. No, you may take his body now. I have your address to mail the death certificate on your admittance paperwork. I will send you the bill as well.

ED. We are a poor ranch and will need to make payments.

DOCTOR. I can arrange for this.

ED. Thank you.

He and Ben pick up their father's body, his arms across his chest covered by his big black hat. Jessie is followed by her daughters, wrapped in their reservation blankets. They get to the wagon. William's body is placed between Jessie and his daughters. Ben and Ed get up on the buckboard. Ben will be driving the wagon this time back to the ranch. There will be no rush, no danger from bad roads. This is not the outcome that any of them had been hoping for. When they've returned to their ranch, they are greeted by Albert and Lucy. They had volunteered to watch all of William and Jessie's grandchildren.

> ED, *to Albert.* Dad is dead. He died of what they are
> now calling the Spanish Flu and pneumonia.

> ALBERT. Well, you know my thoughts are with
> you and your family. I'm going to miss him.

> ED. Dad gave me his watch at the last minute.
> Look.

He shows the watch and then the locket attached to the fob.

> ED. See? The locket opens up.

He opens it, and there is the picture of Oliver and Mary and William and Jessie.

> ALBERT. I remember him showing it to me after
> his marriage to your mom. He got the photo
> special for the occasion. It was a remembrance
> of his family, both past and present. And so now
> it is yours, the future.

Lucy and Jessie are hugging, and the daughters have all begun to cry again. Ben has driven the wagon into the barn to take care of the horses. His dad's corpse is still in the middle of the wagon. Eventually, his body is taken inside and the women prepare his body on the kitchen table. The death song is sung over his body, and friends are invited over to grieve with the family and to say their last goodbyes.

In two days, his body is buried in the family plot at Kirby. So many family members are there. William and Jessie have left a legacy that continues to today. Ed is at the funeral, his watch in his pocket. At the end of the funeral, he pulls the watch out, looks at the time, and places it back into his pocket.

ED, *in a whisper*. Thanks, Dad. You did good.

After William's Death

- Colonel Cyrus Aaron Bixby married Catharine, a nurse, and had at least one child, William. He died September 28, 1916, in Terre Haute, Indiana, in a veteran's home.
- Jackson Leander Bixby married Mary C. They lived in the Indian Territory that became Oklahoma. He died January 15, 1934, and is buried in Muscatine County, Iowa.
- Elizabeth Bixby lived in a poor house in 1870 but went to live with her brother Aaron. She never married.
- Lewis Martin Bixby married Elizabeth Curry and had ten children. He died January 13, 1932, in Muscatine, Iowa.
- Sallie Harris died February 23, 1932, on the Northern Cheyenne Indian Reservation. She was eighty-one years old.
- Jessie Bixby died May 16, 1940, on the Northern Cheyenne Indian Reservation. She was eighty-seven years old.
- Edward Bixby married Elenor Kelsey, and they had twelve children. Their descendants include the grandchildren of the author, Cynthia Drayer. He died January 1981 in Sheridan, Wyoming, at the age of ninety-four.

- Lucy Spang had thirteen children with Albert Spang. After Wolfert was born, she had Sarah Jane, Harriet S, Edith Cordelia, and Kash John ("Buster"). She died April 1, 1934, in Lame Deer, Montana, at sixty-five, and Albert died January 7, 1937, at the age of eighty-one.
- Jack Flagg and Imogene (Spang) gave up ranching and moved into Buffalo, Wyoming. He became a publisher for the Voice newspaper. They had five children together. He died October 14, 1925, in Reno, Nevada.
- Alonzo Taylor, Jack's stepson, married Anna Peterson and had nine children. He died July 14, 1923, in Idaho.
- Walter Reed, son of Oliver and Mary Adaline (Bixby) Reed, married three times: to Roslind Converse, with whom he had six children; to Polly Ann Kelley, with four children; and to Nancy Conover. He died March 24, 1952.
- After Nate Champion's death part of the KC ranch (which was later to become the city of KayCee), was sold to the grandfather of President Gerald Ford.
- The TA Ranch is still a place of interest, and people go to see the fortified barn that still stands today.
- Concerning the Sand Creek Massacre almost 150 years after the incident, a settlement was finally made in 2013 between the US government and the survivors of the Sand Creek Massacre. All descendants of Humpback Woman / Josie received compensation.

Jessie Chasaway (1853 - 1940) and William Bixby (1845 - 1918) taken 1914 at their ranch in Kirby, Montana

William "George" Harris (1849 - 1901) - married Sallie Shell, half sister to Jessie Bixby

Sallie (Shell) Harris (1850-1932), :(Spottedtail/Woostaa; Nickname: Vehiogaha - Little white girl), half sister to Jessie Chasaway

Lucy (Vino museae) ((Cahill/Harris) Spang (1858 - 1934), wearing a blouse and skirt with elk teeth decoration. Daughter of Sallie Harris

Alban ("Albert") Dumont Spang (1855 - 1937) -
Married Lucy Harris, Jessie's neice

Marriage Certificate of Alban Spang and Lucy (Cahill/
Harris), 25 Dec 1885, Canyon Ranch, Crazy Woman
Creek, near Buffalo, Johnson County, Wyoming

Spang Farm

Lucy Spang with daughters, (L to R)- Front: Hattie, Edith;
Middle: Sarah; Back: Katy (Kittie), Nellie, Julia

Walter Reed (1859 - 1950) son of Oliver Hazzard Perry
Reed and Mary Adaline Bixby - William's nephew

Edward John Bixby (1886 - 1981) and his wife, Elenor ("Nora") Kelsey
(1904 - 1977), Son of William and Jessie

Corporal Cyrus "Aaron" Bixby (1840 - 1916),
Civil War Veteran, brother of William

Lewis Martin Bixby (1854 - 1932), brother of William

Indian Funerary Platform

Black Kettle (Moke-tav-a-to), Southern Cheyenne "Peace" Chief
(@1813 - 1868), step son to Humpback Woman. Killed at the massacre of
Wachita River by the 7th cavalry under Gen. George Armstong Custer

Sand Creek Massacre (November 29, 1864) - Lindneaux Painting

Col. John M. Chivington, Courtesy of the Colorado
Historical Society. - he led the Sand Creek Massacre

Wachita River Massacre (11/27/1868) led by Gen. George
Armstong Custer -- 50 women and children were taken
hostage - This is where Black Kettle was killed.

Mary (Day) Harwood House, Vicksburg, Warren Co., MS

Marry Harwood House showing cannon used
in Civil War Siege of Vicksburg, MS

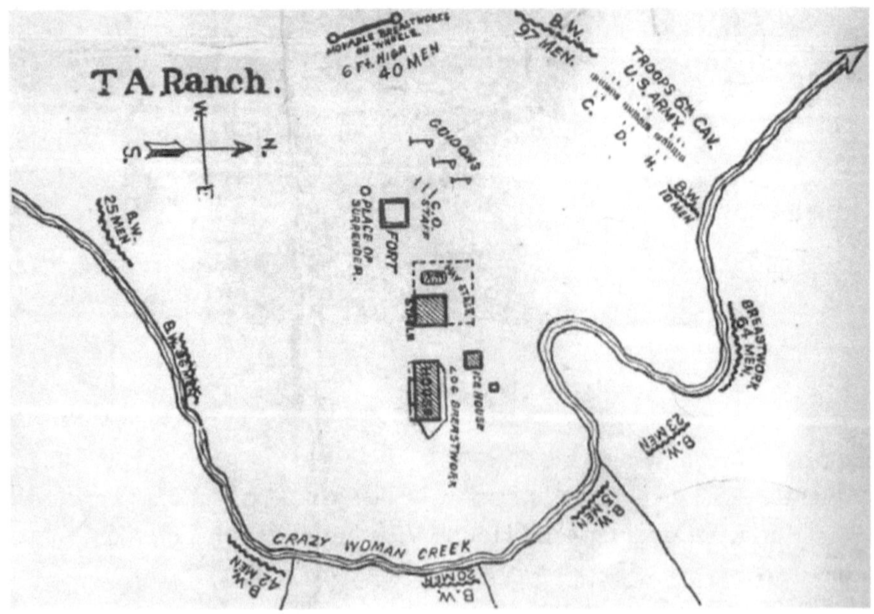

TA Ranch - Plan of attack by public posse around the 50
Regulators from Texas, 1892, Johnson Co., WY

Breastwork to be used at the TA Ranch to force the Regulators out.

TA Ranch Stable - where the Regulators hid from the posse

KC Ranch - where Nate Champion was murdered by the Regulators.
Later purchased by President Gerald Ford's ancestor.

Regulators (AKA: the Invaders) - Taken to Cheyenne,
WY, after they were captured at the TA Ranch

Nate Champion - (1857 - 1892) murdered by
the Regulators on Apr. 9, 1892

Ella Watson (AKA: Cattle Kate) - (1860 - 1889) wrongly
hung for cattle rustling on July 20, 1889

Bar C Cattle Wagon (WSA Sub Neg 12128) - wagon for cattle roundup - includes Nate Champion and Jack Flagg - @1884 (Jack Flagg was a brother-in-law to Albert Spang and Step father to Alonzo Taylor))

Maria "Imogene" (Spang) Taylor/Flagg (1858 - 1937) - wife of Jack Flagg, sister of Albert Spang and mother of Alonzo Taylor

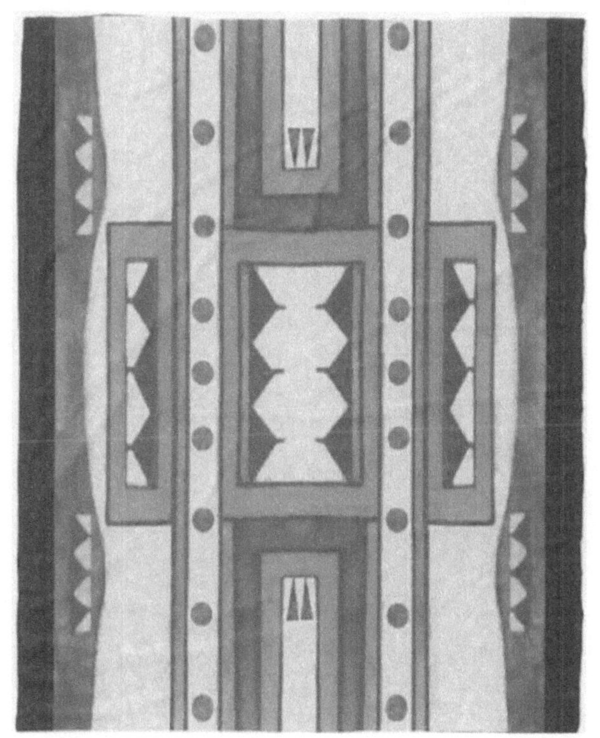

Example of Cheyenne Blanket with design from 1860

About the Author

Cynthia Drayer is a longtime amateur genealogist who has enjoyed researching family lines for both herself and for her friends. Both she and her biological mother were adopted at a young age. She was able to reconnect with her mother and eventually located her living aunts and uncles. With the help of DNA analysis, she was able to determine who her biological father was and has connected with her brothers and sisters.

She has a Bachelor of Science degree in Geology from Portland State University. She worked for thirty-seven years for the State of Oregon helping teen parents obtain their high school diplomas or GEDs. She has two children and three grandchildren, who live in Portland, Oregon, with her.